D1168354

The Basket Maker

The Basket Maker

A NOVEL

By
Kate Niles

CALCASIEU PARISH PUBLIC LIBRARY
LAKE CHARLES, LOUISIANA 70601

GREYCORE PRESS

Copyright © 2004 by Kate Niles

Designed by Kathleen Massaro
Jacket Art by Paul Keskey

Niles, Kate Fuller.
  The basket maker : a novel / by Kate Niles
  p. cm.
  LCCN 2003115806
  ISBN 0-9742074-0-3

  1. Child abuse—Fiction. 2. Four Corners
Region—Fiction. 3. Ute Indians—Fiction.
4. Ouray—Fiction. 5. Basket weaving—Fiction.
I. Title.

PS3564.1377B37 2004   813'.54
                                       QB133-1749

For Christopher

Acknowledgements

Many thanks to Joan Schweighardt, who believed in this book from the get-go and hung onto the idea of its publication for a very long time; my mentors at Vermont College: Francois Camoin, Christopher Noel, and Sharon Sheehe-Stark, all three of whom opened my eyes and taught me how to structure a novel, as well as Sena Jeter Naslund, who read the first pages of an early draft and graced me with her uncanny ability to read works on precisely their own terms; Sergeant Doug Embree of the Durango Police Department for information on probable cause and search warrant procedures; Dan Koenig of Pagosa Springs, former burn unit nurse, for accuracy regarding burn patients and their hospital experiences; the Good Old Girls—Marsha, Maurine, Susan, Linda, Jo—who healed me and continue to heal me; the countless very brave women and men who have dared to come forward about incest and other forms of childhood sexual abuse; my many good friends through the years; and my husband Jonathan and my son Chris for teaching me the meaning of long-term, genuine love.

Alas, where is the guide, that fond virgin,
Ariadne, to supply the simple clue that will
give us courage to face the Minotaur, and the
means then to find our way to freedom when
the monster has been met and slain?

—JOSEPH CAMPBELL

The sky and timbered mountain see you.
If you believe this, you will grow old.

—LUISENO INDIAN SAYING

Part One

Earthsong

We've been here for several billion years, shape-shifting as the gods worked their ways on us, folding us and making us molten and then hard, and finally burping us up from the belly of this Earth until we became what the pale two-leggeds down below call peaks. It's a recent name, peak, given only a hundred-odd years ago, which is the blink of a bothered eye by our standards. Knots of us they call by names like the La Plata Mountains and The Needles; the whole lot of us they call the San Juans.

The recent two-leggeds are remarkably powerful. They call themselves people, but from our standpoint when one of them climbs close enough what we notice first is how they can't maneuver like the bighorn sheep or the small picas, but stand upright to free their front paws for other work. The recent two-leggeds have scrambled up here more than others in the past, and we've felt their drills and hammers.

There were two-leggeds before this, of course, browner and fewer in number, and without possession of the noisy machines capable of digging up our rock, or of flying, or of chopping down meadow grass. The brown two-leggeds had names for us too, but these names have gone, and the snow geese say the brown two-leggeds are relegated now to lands south of here. They're very poor and have lost just about everything. It's a worry, say the snow geese, it's a worry. But the geese also say that the brown two-leggeds can still see us, and so if they can find their way to us and want to, they will still know how to pray.

A glacier cut us badly not so long ago, and after it receded it left a river valley lined with our remnants and those of red stone and shale. A fifty-mile valley, to go by the measurements of the white two-leggeds, and up it they run something called a train. It's quite sweet, really—there is no other word. A black, belching engine, a coal box, then a line of neat yel-

low cars carrying passengers to and fro. Coal trains used to run up and down the valley too, but we haven't seen those for a while now. At the southern end of the valley is the town of La Plata; at the north, the town of Coalton. La Plata is 6,500 feet in elevation; Coalton 10,000. The snow geese say there's a college now in La Plata, and tourism from the train, and some ranching still in the surrounding countryside.

The snow geese say the white two-leggeds are increasingly odd. Or, perhaps, as they've always struck us as odd (the machinery that guts whatever it touches, the women in clothing too restrictive for climbing), they're now odd in unfamiliar ways. They're fighting a war in a far-off land and killing their sons for no apparent reason. Their leader, a president, is under investigation for sabotaging his opponents in secretive and cowardly ways. And their children sleep at night down long hallways from their parents, and their parents do not come when they wake up from nightmares. Worst of all, the parents sometimes cause the nightmares.

What do you mean? we ask the geese of this last. But the geese just shudder. We have work to do, they say. That is all they say.

Down Below

SARAH

Silence. Me and Ricky lie in our basement bedroom, by ourselves, the first room we've had to share in our whole life. We don't get why this has to be the case, but when they bought the house Mom and Dad were full of the big basement and how we could have the run of it. Problem is, it's not finished, and the black widows own it. There's two perfectly good rooms upstairs but Mom wants both of them. Kind of piggy of her, though if we ask to move upstairs, we're the ones who're called piggy.

Over on his bed Ricky's scowling. I decide he doesn't want to be pestered, so I don't try to talk to him. It's a cold October and we're still getting used to the new school. We moved here in June. It's the fourth time we've moved, and I'm only ten.

We sit here with our noses in books until we hear Mom on the stairs, moving toward the laundry. When she comes in with a full clothesbasket, Ricky leaves, and I finally ask why we move so much. I have to ask quick because I know she'll only stay long enough to sort our clothes, not hers and Dad's, and then go back upstairs.

It scares me a little to ask. You never know about Mom. She might be okay with a question, or she might think I'm complaining, when all I want is to know something. This time, though, Mom laughs and jokes that she and Dad are itinerant professors, Tom Joads of the academic world. It's been tough for the past few years, she says. Since 1970, when the Ph.D. market dried up.

"What's Tom Joad?" I ask. Ricky's gone to the den and has the TV on, so I have to speak up a little. I've heard all about Ph.D.s, but not about Tom Joad.

"*Who* is Tom Joad. Who, you mean. He's a character in John Steinbeck's *Grapes of Wrath*. It's a novel about people moving West in the Depression."

"You mean kind of like Dad's family?"

Mom's eyes waver at me, the way they do when she's not sure she wants to admit to something. I sink a little inside. Her mood shifts so quick sometimes. She snaps a shirt. "Sort of. Only the Graves weren't Okies. They were from Nebraska. And they were better educated."

"Oh." I decide not to talk anymore.

Who is Tom Joad. I can never say anything without some correction coming. Who is Tom Joad. I think about the next time I'll visit the library. I'll read a little, sitting there on the floor with the book open, blocking the aisle so that people have to step over me. I'll learn who Tom Joad is, and then put the book back on the shelves. I might think about checking it out, but it'll probably look too big and hard and so I'll skip to my favorites—Nancy Drew, Laura Ingalls Wilder, biographies for kids.

This town's got a good library. This is the third Rocky Mountain town we've lived in. I love the Rockies. We just did a unit in school on Chief Ouray and the Utes, and I pretend I'm a Ute girl half the time now. The first town, where I was born, was in the South, but Mom and Dad only lived there a year and I don't remember any of it. I was too young to read books then, anyway.

When Mom's done with the laundry and disappears upstairs, I'm left with the concrete and spiders. The black widows rule the corners. Me and Ricky hate to admit it, but we're afraid of stepping on them at night. Dad sprays but it doesn't do much good. He holds a metal can in one hand and a stiff hose-like thing in the other, and puts this nasty-smelling stuff all over the place.

Outside our door is a hall. To the right, the stairs go up, and past that, it opens into the garage where Dad's got his workbenches and tools. He has this brown board full of holes in it that he hangs on the wall. He hangs hooks in the holes and his tools on the hooks. He's very picky about his tools and tells us never to touch them. When he's making something—bookshelves, mostly, because both Mom and him have a ton of books—he's very concentrated and tight. Like a spring wound up. His biceps bulge and his T-shirt stretches across his back so you can see his muscles working, and he holds his mouth as if the rows of his teeth are two parts of a puzzle snapped together.

I want him to stop being so wound up. Jaw so tight. What makes him happy is not Mom or Ricky or our house. But it might be me if I can just be like one of his students he hangs around with so much. Sometimes, when it's just us two, I can make his eyes brighten the way they do when Ike or Peter come visit, or the way they did in the last place we lived, with his students then—Steve Rye and Doug Wilson. I do this—make him light up—by cracking a joke like the ones they crack. ("Dad, why did the cowboy buy a dachshund?" "Why?" "Because he was told to get a long little doggie!") And then he'll laugh, tipping his head back so that his thin lips stretch and soon all I see are small rows of teeth, like piano keys, and his chin jutting out. Then he brings his head down and the moment's over. But it's enough. It's enough to let me know that if I just work it right, I can win his heart as much as any of those boys he teaches.

The black widows give us an idea.

"Let's make a web," Ricky says.

"A spider web?"

"Duh. What other kind?"

"Thought you hated widows." I poked one once so it would roll over and I could show him the red hourglass on its belly. He about had a heart attack.

"I didn't say a widow web. Just a general web."

"Okay," I say, and we seem to know exactly what we're both talking about even though we haven't talked about it at all. Upstairs, we take some string from the gift-wrapping drawer, also scissors and tape. We go back down and start in the corner opposite the door, then pull a string in from all the other corners. Four Corners. Just like the monument not that far from here, a couple of hours, where me and Ricky and Dad stopped on a trip once this past summer. Mom doesn't like camping or driving very much, so in the summers we go places without her. This is another way to make Dad almost happy. Go out with him, like he does with his students, and fart around outside. He doesn't ever take us backpacking (the real way to be in the wilderness), but he will take us to see national parks and go camping.

I loved visiting the Four Corners Monument. You could have a foot in Utah and Arizona at the same time, put your hands down to cover New Mexico and Colorado. Kind of like State Twister. And if you lifted your head you could see in all directions, the red desert going on forever, all bluffs and sun. A few Navajos set up ramadas nearby, selling earrings and fry bread and Cokes, but other than that there's just some Port-a-Potties squatting out in the sun, and the road in. Way out, middle of nowhere. An X made up for no reason. A cross in the sand. No rivers or mountain ranges showed that there should be four states meeting there, but there they were. As if somebody-or-other explorer type played God one day, pointed a finger, and drew the lines out. Crazy.

I pull the Arizona string in from the corner in that direction, southwest. Ricky runs in the New Mexico one, from the southeast. He holds the two together in the center while I tack Utah to the corner and walk toward Ricky. Finally, Colorado, the one by the door, the state where we are, the one I want, all of a sudden, stronger than any other line. I can't say why, except my heart's going a hundred miles a minute and I feel the way Mom acts when a truck passes us on the highway and she freaks out. I hate feeling this way. I hate being a wimp like her. But still, I wish that string were thick as a ski tow, or better yet, see-through but really strong, like fishing wire. Yeah, that's good, fishing wire.

Ricky ties the states together. Now we have our own Four Corners Monument in the middle of the room. Five feet high, maybe, as high as Ricky's arms will reach, halfway between the light on the ceiling and the concrete floor.

But the four strings by themselves will not stop a thing. So we let the Monument droop while we weave strings around and around, spiders making our nest. What was that Greek goddess spider? Ariadne? Was that it? Are we Ariadne? Or Spider Woman, like the Navajo have. I think Spider Woman is better. I mean, the Navajo Reservation spills into three of the Four Corners states. But does Spider Woman weave? Mrs. Lovato at school seems to think she just warns the Hero Twins about their father. That's good, but mainly I want Spider Woman to weave; she has to weave—she's a spider. I wonder if the Utes have Spider Woman too. The Utes ran around all these states as well. I love Indians and it's important to know who all and what all went on in the place where I live.

We create a new world in our room. Once the web is up we put a stick up in the middle to make it all taut. The room now has the gray cement walls, the two kids' beds under the web across and zigzag from each other, and the white web. That's all there is, just a cell-like space, because Ricky and me refuse to really move into this room by putting up posters or spilling toys. We even refuse to take the web down when Halloween passes; it snows a foot that night and we can't go trick-or-treating anyway.

Not that I expected much in the way of trick-or-treating. Dad would've had to drive us, as the houses are spaced too far apart here. But I did sort of want to knock on the neighbor's door to the north. Old Oodegaard's door. I've seen Mrs. Oodegaard. Fat lady, very old and very fat.

"Hey Ricky," I say that night, the snow falling, eating the candy Mom gave us to make up for no trick-or-treating.

"What, Sarah?" He unwraps a lollipop, and sucks it into his mouth.

"They say the neighbor-lady's husband hung himself in the base-ment."

"What? Who says that?"

"That big girl on the bus."

"How does she know?"

"She just does."

Ricky scowls at me. He's always scowling these days. "Why do you always want to know that stuff?" he asks. "Why? What's wrong with you?"

I don't answer. Ricky wads up his candy bag and flails at Spider Woman's string, cussing, as he heads for the door. He barely glances at me, and then he's gone.

I exhale into the silence. It's always silent. *No one ever talks.*

MADDY

Tonight a deer stands silhouetted in the bright light the Graves keep on in their yard at night. The deer come visit in fall and winter, and I have to squint to see that it is in fact deer and not elk out on that field of snow. The elk usually graze down in the floodplain this time of year, scratching for food through drifts and icy crusts.

The Graves are my neighbors, and behind all of the houses that string out along this river valley lies a rugged ridge of red stone, slant-ing toward heaven or hell depending upon your frame of mind, and mantled with pinon and ponderosa and scrub oak. When it's not so snowy I sometimes see the little Graves girl hopping the low stone wall that divides their civilized back yard grass from the spill of the wild mountain. She hops in what looks like an old nightgown of her mother's that she's got cinched around her waist, and she takes the dog along with her. The dog is a big German Shepherd—purebred, it looks like to me—and the way she treats it I figure she's pretend-ing it's a horse. She straddles it, trying to ride, but she always slips off when the dog begins walking. So she just calls him—Beowulf is his name—and up the mountain they go. I have no idea what she does up there, but the old nightgown and the horse-dog make me think she's playing Pioneer Girl.

The deer nuzzles the ground. I sigh. I was a pioneer girl once. Madeleine Marie Larsen, before I became Madeleine Larsen Oodegaard. I'm well past seventy now, sleepless at night, which is how I see the deer silhouetted in the spotlight. It's a Christmas-y show of wildlife, and at some point the deer always stands stalk-still, ears cocked as if it's listening intently. I wonder what it hears, what it knows, what secrets the mountains are telling it in the occasional drip of snow off branches, the far yip of a coyote, the way a light in the Graves' basement shimmers through the low windows after midnight.

Why the light stays on in the Graves' basement is beyond me, but it's on again tonight. My eyes aren't very good anymore, so I have to squint into those narrow seams of yellow running close to the ground. I see shadows; once I thought I saw the little girl. Otherwise, nothing, though at two a.m. one time I did hear a door close outside and I had to wonder what that was all about too. I can't sleep because things in my own house spook me, and the light on at the Graves' spooks me too.

I've lived two miles outside of this town, up this crack of a river valley, for forty-odd years. Lars quit his father's homestead in '22 and we moved out here, first to the Philistine Mine, and then thirty miles down the valley to here, to this little white cottage outside of La Plata. In '22, Chief Ouray's wife, Chipeta, was still alive and I'd see her sometimes in town. I think of that and realize how long ago it all was.

Soon after we got here, we had the two boys, born up at Philistine, at 9,200 feet. Lars, my husband, worked the mines, but because he had an education (Overton Bible College, Overton, Nebraska), he moved up to mine foreman, and then accounts manager. I was glad when that happened; at least a man a day died in the mines here in Colorado alone.

I attend the First Lutheran Church on Third Avenue. My friend Mildred Carlisle picks me up on Sunday morning at 9:40 sharp, and we drive in. When Lars was alive, we'd go together.

I turn my face away from the Graves' basement window. I can't bear to look at their shadows anymore, the sinister stretch of light. The deer bolts, and all I see are Lars' feet swinging in my own basement, the chair kicked out from under him.

SARAH

My dad puts his stuff away in the closet under the basement stairs. He just got back from a backpack trip two weeks ago. He went to a place called The Maze over in Utah. It doesn't have trails for the most part and it's full of really complicated canyons. We'll have a slide show in about a week when he gets the slides developed and then he'll show us pretty pictures of blooming prickly pear, and of course a few geology shots. My dad's pretty good with a camera, and I like what he likes—the mountains and rocks and canyons. He doesn't take pictures of Indian ruins, though, and those are my favorites.

He packs everything in little baggies before setting off on one of these trips. When he's getting ready with the baggies he whistles under his breath and is springy. He pulls his pack out of the closet and everything's just so. Just so just so just so. Small boxes of waterproof matches. Toilet paper in a plastic bag, matchbook inside the squashed tube. A snake bite kit; gorp he put together himself from M&Ms, raisins, nuts, dried banana slices. Freeze-dried cheesecake. Pans nested into one another, all encased in a nylon stuff sack. Sleeping bag squeezed into the smallest sack possible, choked together with a sleeping pad by two cinch straps at the bottom of his pack. Dad and Ike actually got into a debate about whether to use twist ties for the baggies or just knot them. Dad says he won, for now: "Twist ties are just more garbage you're likely to miss packing out."

And off he would go, like that, with Ike and Peter this last time, or, in the last place, with Steve and Doug. Different college, different boys. Off he would go. Out the door, footstep light and bouncy, the car full of his stuff. He doesn't know it, but my heart trips after him, until the dust from the car driving off has settled a bit. And then it's all alone there in the driveway, my heart, a little red thing beating *why don't I make you springy, why can't I go*, until I grab it back, seal it up inside me again, and go read a book.

Pull, pull it tighter from the north wall, the wall my bed's against, the wall toward Oodegaard's. The web's sagging there. We leave it up, the web, because it usually works.

I just want to make you happy.

He comes back from this Fall Trip the way he comes back from all these trips, smelly and smiling. We're glad to see him. But he takes a shower and shaves and eats Mom's hamburgers and then I see the jaw start to straighten out again, clenching, and his shoulders get heavy. It's like he's doing his duty, being here. Standing guard or something. I don't understand it. Why'd he get married and have us if it's such a drag?

Each day he gets a little more clammed up, the shoulders stooping like Grandma's, the lawn and the spider-spraying and bookshelf-making all sort of one big *obligation* (Mrs. Lovato had that as a bonus on our vocabulary this week). He and Mom go back to reading, silent, at night in their own chairs in the living room. We hide out under the web. And a few times, I hear some thrashing, s*hit* under his breath, some kind of huffing that soaks into my dreams. But when I wake up all I can hear is my heart going too loud, pounding in the dead black.

At school in November, right before Thanksgiving, a boy named Trent plays kickball on the younger kids' playground and falls down below into an open manhole. I don't know about it at all till the next day when he makes the front page of the paper. I read the newspaper all the time, and God there he is. Trent MacIntosh, bandaged.

Trent's in fourth grade. He kicks the ball past the infield and runs. Being a boy, he'll run really fast because he doesn't usually get off a good kick like this and he wants to score. He runs and runs, until it's too late and the hole stares up at him like some kind of really bad joke.

I have to make it to second base. He'll think that. Staring at the black circle like an animal at headlights, leaping at the same time, taking a flying pitch over the edge of the open manhole. But he hasn't had any time to get up a special speed to jump over it, or to swerve around it. His foot slips on the far edge. His ankle twists and crushes into the hole. His body follows.

The water is so hot it feels cold.

Something inside him shrieks *(shrieks and shrieks, oh yes, I know this part),* and then he remembers only some distant cries of his name and a bunch of hands, like snowflakes in a bad wind, coming in at him before everything else is lost.

Where am I? Where am I? he must think now. Fluorescent light, a weird feeling that he can't move.

Galveston, I read in the papers. They had to fly "the MacIntosh boy" to Galveston for skin grafts. Horrible pictures of the faces of burned children stare out at me from the Sunday pull-out section. The newspaper is doing a special story because of Trent's accident. Over sixty-five percent of Trent's body has suffered second and third degree burns. People are raising money for his treatment. His parents are suing the school. Why was the manhole cover left off after lunch, all the hot dishwater from the lunch dishes steaming below? Who would be so stupid?

I'm almost sorry I missed the tragedy. I wasn't a hundred yards away, on the other side of the building where the fifth graders play. I grill Ricky, who's in fourth grade like Trent. *Where were you? Did you see it?*

No. He was off on the swings at the far end of the playground, swinging up into the peaks, swinging up over the river valley, swinging past the red beds and the train whistle down below and the last of the autumn trees with their shaggy leaves. He says he swings every day. It makes him feel powerful, up there on that mesa, where you can see everything.

But he didn't see Trent fall in.

Galveston? Trent looks at the city paper his dad must be reading at his bedside just the way I'm reading this one. Trent's face was the last thing to hit water, so it remains more or less okay compared to the lower half of his body. He lies wrapped in bandages. The pain is terrible, but dull. His whole being would feel dulled, like the time someone, his mom probably, would have given him cough syrup laced with codeine. An IV drips into his arm. He knows it's an IV from TV shows he's seen. He must be seriously hurt.

He stares unblinking at his father. He tries to make a noise but nothing happens. His father sees him, folds up the paper, and tries to smile, but his chin wobbles and falls apart instead. Trent's dad can actually cry, unlike mine. Trent's dad doesn't do it very often, though. And his hands shake when they reach to touch Trent's forehead. This scares Trent more than anything else has so far. *Dad? Crying?*

Where is Galveston?

They take pig skin and graft it onto his legs and abdomen. "Pig skin is remarkably like human skin, and is very resilient in grafting operations," states the doctor in the newspaper. The Galveston hospital specializes in kids with burns. They flew Trent there from La Plata in a helicopter. The paper said it was as if the whole municipal airport stopped breathing when Trent was loaded on. No one played the only pinball machine in the corner. No other aircraft took off. Pilots removed their hats for the kid in the stiff white bandages, an oxygen mask on his face, an IV following him aboard. Even the

Pioneer Airlines prop jet—going to Denver and by far the biggest thing to land at La Plata—waited for the helicopter to leave.

Everyone breathed a big sigh of relief as it took off, veered southeast, past Chama, over Santa Fe. It flew out onto the huge Staked Plain of west Texas, where I read that the first Spanish men—Coronados—once got lost and dreamt about places with no landmarks, no ups or downs, no mountains or hills in the distance. Just an endless, grassy, windblown pancake.

Only the birds really know how to navigate there without help from dials and such. I close my eyes and see the snow geese that come through Colorado in the fall. They fly very high and know where they are going when they migrate. They avoid the Plain if they can help it. The day Trent took off, the geese clucked and pecked at marsh weeds on their refuge along the river. It was afternoon. Trent was being rescued. I was riding home on the bus. A little thump hit my chest, a wing flutter. I reached for it, that flutter. Nothing made me feel safer. I reached for it.

But the geese were too far away.

MADDY

I fold the paper and glance out the window toward the Graves' place. I'm done reading about that ridiculous war President Nixon continues to wage. I've never been so ashamed of being a Republican in all my life. I was willing to withhold my judgments until Kent State, but when a nation kills its own children there is no excuse.

So I'm done. Done reading about Nixon, done reading letters to the editor debating about whether or not to establish the Philistine Wilderness Area, done aching for the ninth day in a row over Barbara MacIntosh's boy. It pesters me, that ache, because I've known Barbara since she was a little girl. We've lost contact over the years, but I remember her. Of all the children I've taught in Sunday School, Barbara's one of a handful who stick out. She was always doing things with her hands, weaving potholders and God's Eyes and knitting sweaters for dolls.

So I have to call her. Soon. I would hardly know how to do this except for having to call Ted and Walter after their father killed—died—but even with that experience it's hard.

I bank the fire in the woodstove and smooth the newspaper once again in front of me. Trent's sweet little face reappears, covered with bandages, a smile trying to brew. I stroke an old arrowhead I found a long time ago and shake my head. Boiled lobster, just like boiled lobster. That's what John LeTourneau said when I was little and I overheard him telling my mother about a railroad accident, where somebody released steam without looking and cooked a man's face. LeTourneau was the only person in western Nebraska from Maine, and he said his A's as broad as a board.

SARAH

"I want to meet Trent."

"Why?"

"Because I just want to."

Ricky shrugs and goes back to playing with fake money. He calls his game Joe Businessman. He gets sucked into his business games the way I do playing Pioneer Girl. Both games mean you need to be totally alone. So I leave Ricky and go back to my side of the room.

We're working on Mom for upstairs rooms (finally!) because it's too cold down here. It isn't like Mom's heart is warming up or anything. Okay okay, it's too cold, she says. She sighs this over toast in the kitchen a week before the Trent thing. Old nightgown, longer now in early winter. That's good because in the summer she wears these short flimsy things you can see right through and her body just overtakes us. Ricky hates it worse than I do.

"Isn't she getting any?" he asks.

Like he knows. But he does. *Playboy* up there in the tree house with his friend Kyle up the road. Nine years old, and he knows.

I got to try sleeping upstairs one night, and I thought next to

Mom and Dad's bedroom would feel safer because then Mom might be more aware of things, but all it really does is make me feel funny. There's something gross about picturing the two of them together, Mom oozing and hating herself, Dad *obliged* and his voice dry as grass rubbing on dust—

But the only one who gets mad in public, at all, is Ricky. He's so rude and he bangs things. When does Dad get mad? Mom? There's a volcano between them that never blows, at least not to each other. Not out loud. It goes somewhere else, and sometimes I can feel their hot lava creeping all over me, like what Trent must have felt like when the water soaked into his skin.

MADDY

I should call Barbara. I must call Barbara. But my hands feel cold, my insides weak. My hand stops as soon as I put my right index finger into the hole for dialing. I had to look up her number in the phone book, for goodness' sake. How well do I know her anymore? Isn't she a—what do they call that?—a textile artist now? What is that? A fancy word for weaver?

Does it matter, Maddy? Where is your Christian good sense? And why don't you go introduce yourself to the new neighbors? Bring by some lemon bars for those kids?

Something frosty about that mother, though. That's why.

Never stopped you before, Oodegaard. Why the fears now?

I sag. Take my finger out of the phone. Lars, I think. *Lars! You are leaving my mind, Lars!*

And before I know it, tears form in the spaces behind my eyes.

SARAH

I hate it that Mom doesn't see us, and sometimes I almost cry. I look at the newspaper photo of Trent and see the back of what must be his mom, her hand reaching out to his. Trent's looking at her, too, not at the camera. I stare and stare at their hands touching. I want that.

The afternoons are too endless. Mom's not working even though she has a Ph.D. from Princeton. She snorts that the college here thinks she's "just a faculty wife" and won't hire her. But even with all her free time she still doesn't pay much attention to us.

The nearest kids are a half a mile away. There are two across the street, but their family is strange. They are bible thumpers, and bible thumpers always talk about sin and make me feel bad.

I see Mrs. Oodegaard out waddling in her garden, and we almost smile at each other one day. But she seems sad and I'm shy about any old lady I don't know very well, 'specially one with a husband who hung himself.

The oak leaves are down and brown. They skitter along our patio. Everything smells musty and old and dry. Autumn.

I think about Trent. I read every story the paper runs about burns, about fires. I sleep upstairs now, not that it helps. At night, when the thing Mom doesn't see, the Something with the eely fingers and sandpaper chin doesn't happen, doesn't take me downstairs again, I listen hard to the furnace go on in the basement. I wonder if Mrs. Oodegaard listens to her basement like this. Once, when I got brave enough to sit up, I thought I saw a light on over there.

Each click of heat noise makes my heart pound. The house must be burning down. *No, it can't be. Go see.* No. I squint in the dark. *That lump on the chair looks like a monster. No. Go see.* I get up, check the lump. Clothing, nothing more. I open my door a crack. Heart thumping. *What if he's there?* But he's not there tonight. I go to the top of the stairs. The furnace is at the bottom of them. I stare and stare at the blue flame of the pilot light. The furnace goes on, goes off. Goes on. I match noises with the actions of the furnace, memorize them so I'll know when I am lying in bed, listening, exactly what is happening. I'll know what is normal and what is not normal. I'll know what to tell Trent when I finally get to meet him; will know to say, *I know what it's like to be on fire, even though the house never burned down like that.*

Indian

I finally dial Barbara's number, even if it is three in the afternoon, and if I'm honest with myself I'll admit I'm calling at a time when she's not likely to be home. School gets out at three in the afternoon; no doubt she'll be picking up her younger boy. No doubt, too, she'll be wanting to stay out of that silent house, with no husband and no older boy. The papers say Trent's father went with him to Galveston. I wonder why. Why him and not her?

I couldn't bear it, I know. Having a son that scalded. Maybe Trent Sr. can deal with it better. Maybe.

The phone rings and rings. No answer. I put the phone down and stroke the agate arrowhead. I remember Lars used to say he was haunted by the great Ute Chief Ouray, and I am almost convinced that Ouray owned this arrowhead because it always makes me think of Lars' infatuation. I sometimes think objects carry their histories with them, like auras, or perfume. Not very Christian of me, or only in that strange, séance-y kind of way that ladies of my mother's generation would occasionally go in for.

But I'm sick of ghosts. The house is tight, too close. I go to the back room, what used to be our sons' bedroom that Lars took over for an office when they left home. I lift up the roll top on the desk. More ghosts.

Two old postcards, illustrations of Ouray and his wife, Chipeta, stare up at me. A few books on religions of the world. An ancient prescription for Lithium that I could rarely get Lars to take. Oh Lord. If he had taken it? If he had...? They say Ouray's body is lost somewhere up this valley. That his tribesmen never got him to his proper burial home. They say. They say if Lars had taken his Lithium he might not have…might not have… Oh Lord, how could I have helped him any more than I did, so that he might not have died?

I swear Ouray winks at me from his sepia postcard. I slam the roll top back down and leave the room.

OURAY

Here I am, a skeleton since 1880, dead ninety-some winters up this hillside and I'm still upset over President Grant. I told him and that Congress to their face that they would not get to our people, that they underestimated us, but they did not listen. They sat there and gazed at me the way their fat cows always gaze, and one of them actually said to me, "Look, Ouray, you and your Utes had nothing but bows and arrows until the European came along. Underestimate you?"

How could I reply to someone who could not have made a knife from stone to save his life, who had no notion even of what kind of rock it might take, or if it needed fire-treating to harden it, and certainly not the details of actually making the thing, flake by flake? So I just stared at him, at all their ridiculous shirts stuffed with ascots, at their shiny boots, at the snuff dandruff sneaking out of their front pockets. This was after their war, their "civil" war (there is no such thing as a civil war, but the whites will convince themselves of anything). They slaughtered one another and left their beat-up soldiers to come out west and pick up where they left off.

And they did underestimate me. They underestimated even the enemies of my people, the Lakota and the Arapaho. I hate to admit this about my enemies, because when he was five they stole my only son, my beautiful Paron. But it was my fault, losing him. My fault because I took my son out with me to the Plains, where our enemies were. And my fault later, much later, when the government mistook me for a weakling but still got whatever it wanted. It is painful to know how much power you have, and still be trampled to death.

My wife, Chipeta, came after I'd been dead a long time and told me that all the newspapers had written obituaries telling that I, Chief Ouray, had been "the greatest Indian of his time" and a man of "pure instincts, of keen perception, and apparently possessed of very proper ideas of justice and right." I laughed in her face. She knew for sure then that I hadn't gone on to the Spirit World. She laughed too, and together our bitter laughter rang over the countryside. I'd been peering up at the stars for twenty years then, twenty years of knowing what season it was by the turn of the Great Dipper, who pours the stars out each night.

"Would you like to look down for a change?" she asked. I was surprised. Maybe it was because she was born Apache that death didn't scare her as much as it did Utes. But it took her twenty years to come back so I thought maybe she was a Ute after all, until that moment when she showed up and started talking to me. I'd missed her so much, but I never lost track of her heart. I never lost track of her heart because she never lost track of mine.

"You know, it is still beautiful here," she said, a little breeze lifting the hair on her forehead. "Do you know where you are?"

Until then I had never been sure, but she rotated my skull gently until I looked out and down, and then I knew I was north out of La Plata, up the river valley on its west side. "There," she said.

Tears filled my eyes. Horses filled the valley. "Put me back—" I tried to tell her, but she had already kissed my eyebrows, and gone.

The horses grazed in the floodplain pastures guarded by barbed wire. I did not look at the wire too hard because it would break my heart. Utes were a horse people above all else. I shifted my eyes downward, to where there were no horses, to the oak thickets and pinons directly below me. That was a long time ago, and I haven't looked up much since.

Recently, things have been moving. Skirts pink as a tongue, with flowers on them. A dog barking. A little girl sweeping at dirt—though for all my experience as Chief, I couldn't say why.

Hah. What could my parents really know about Laura Ingalls Wilder and *Little House on the Prairie*? I like Laura's dad—he likes being a family man. He might be a little obsessed with the frontier and having no neighbors (it's no fun to have to move too much), but at least he likes hanging out with his girls instead of traipsing off into the woods with other people. And I know Laura perfectly. She's a lucky girl with nice parents who gets to meet Mr. Right right away. I would love a life like that. So in the afternoons after school I get out an old nightgown of Mom's that's actually a pretty pink with tiny flowers, belt it around my waist, and ride Beowulf's big shepherd back like a horse for a minute until he wiggles too much. Then I slide off, and crawl into the bushes on the hill behind my house.

I sweep a lot, making home. The hill is not like the forest in fairy tales, with water and swans, and it doesn't look like Laura's prairie full of sloughs and tall grass, either. But it's my favorite. It's rocky, with clumps of scrub oak and pinon. The scrub oak arch from their roots and create hollows. The hollows are floored with smooth dirt underneath, the perfect place for a house. Outside the oak branches, the red rocks and limestone the color of corn make jagged lines that sometimes have quartz crystals in them. I love the crystals; on Saturdays when Dad's messing around in the yard or the garage I take them to him and show him. He says if I look hard I might find big mica chunks too. I like mica. Sheety stuff, peels off like little panes of glass. But he usually doesn't come out and hunt for it with me—he just tells me it's there. It's one more thing I share with Dad that he just doesn't see—a love of rocks. He's a geology professor at La Plata State College.

Don't think about Dad. Not that Dad, so out of it most of the time, his jaw wired shut, putting up with Mom's constant fussing. Just the Dad who makes perfect soups without a recipe, who builds bookshelves so squared you'd never know they didn't come from a real carpenter. Or the Dad who sometimes, in a blue moon, brings a rock back for me from the field, or who takes us to the Four Corners and Mesa Verde National Park in the summers. But not the Dad in love with all his students and not with me. Not that Dad.

I find my favorite smooth patch of dirt and become Laura. Beowulf runs around sniffing at gopher holes and snakeweed, but generally sticks with me, the way a horse would on a pasture out the front door of the homestead. I gather up the nightgown in that really female way women with long skirts always do, with one hand lifting up part of the dress. I just love that—so old-fashioned! I also pretend to have a pretty bun coiled at the base of my neck. I work on cocking it so I'm beautiful, like those old silhouettes of women I see down at the Kittredge Hotel. I imagine that nobody minds me being beautiful. Then I invent a mother and I try to make her like Laura's mom, always canning or quilting or teaching me and my sister Mary to read, or like Trent's mom, holding hands. But it doesn't work for very long, because the mother always gets jealous when I have Pa Ingalls come home, or when my beau visits. I don't understand this.

I drop my skirts, stop curving my neckline. I whack my stick-broom. I shake oak leaves doing it. Whack again. *I want a good mom.* I've torn some leaves. I go stroke them and tell the oak I'm sorry. *What's wrong with me? So mad.* But when the mom thing comes in it's like someone takes an Etch-A-Sketch and shakes out a really fancy drawing someone's worked at a long time.

I close my eyes to reset the picture.

Okay. House, dog-horse, nice rows of canned vegetables, a cozy cabin. Lovely new dress. Okay. Now, send Pa Ingalls out hunting, the way he always did in the books, and have the mother disappear. Okay. Good. That way when Alonzo Wilder shows up, I'm alone.

Alonzo. What a dumb name. It doesn't matter. He loves me. He will marry me. I always play up until then, until the point of being grownup.

Me and Alonzo set up our married house, parents gone for good. Sweep, sweep. *Now what?*

When she stands there down below me looking lost like that, broom stopped in mid-sweep, her playing done so fast I can't look at her, it reminds me of myself, of how life can seem so good and change too quick, the earth cracking open in front of you.

Paron was almost six when I lost him. I was uneasy about it but Chipeta said: Take him out onto the Plains. It's time. He can ride your horses, he is unafraid of elk; it's time for him to face the buffalo.

So Paron and I left Chipeta for the Plains north of Denver with thirty warriors and a dozen women. It was June, and all the rivers were spilling and the grasses were green for the ponies. We stuck to the low passes and made it over easily.

The Plains always confused me at first. If you went far enough east of Denver, you lost the mountains for good, and the first time I went there as a child (when there was no Denver) I realized that without mountains I didn't have a sense of direction. The Cheyenne say that the Plains are the circle of the world. It seems like they find this comforting, as if they were in the center of this circle. In my mind, though, I had no way of telling where the center was. There was just grass and low cliffs I couldn't even see till they rose up at my feet. But after a while, after going back to the same area for many seasons, I started to understand some things. I stayed with the Platte and its side streams for landmarks, and knew where to find buffalo and which cliffs were used to jump them off before we had guns. Sometimes, if we wanted a large amount of meat, we would still use the jumps. The women came along to prepare the meat and hides for carrying; bringing back buffalo across the mountains was a lot of hard work, and the ponies were always tired by the end of it.

Paron was excited, I remember that. He had a wild spirit. The year before, he'd taken my horse, Thunder Cloud, and ridden him even though the horse was wild and Paron didn't have any control. Still, he hung on. He hung on until the horse jabbed him into a tree and ran a limb through his right shoulder. Chipeta dressed his wound and scolded him pretty hard, but the truth was that she was less frightened by his spirit than I was. She was levelheaded and fearless. So when she said, on top of others saying the same thing, Take him to the Plains for his first buffalo hunt, I shut out the visions of buffalo trampling him, of the Lakota sweeping into our camp and stealing our children and horses.

It was a successful hunt. We were happy, our whole party, full of fresh meat and the travois loaded down for the long trip in the morning. The horses grazed next to the river, and the night was clear. Paron had ridden well. His task at that age was just to keep up, to keep up and watch. He lay curled asleep in his blankets, while I sat out front of the tipi to look at the stars. One big advantage to the Plains is that the whole sky is visible.

The fact that I couldn't sleep should have told me something. And the fact that I couldn't keep the ugly visions out of my head—visions of death and stealing, of warriors appearing out of nowhere—should also have told me something. Chipeta always said I had powerful visions, and later she would get angry with me for not listening to them. But she was as powerful as any vision to me, she knew that. And it was she who convinced me to go out there. It is hard sometimes to know what force to listen to when there are two you trust so much.

But in the dark the ground began to shake and I knew it wasn't buffalo running. Soon I made out the sound of horse hooves, then the high scream of the ponies, then the war whoops of the Lakota—a pitch that made my stomach seize.

I should've run for my weapon and away from there, like any man without a child would do. But when they came into camp I sat hackled like a mountain lion defending her cubs. A warrior with slivers of moonlight slicing his eye saw me, read me like fresh deer tracks in the snow. He came on too fast, knocking me over from his horse. He jumped off and crashed through the flap of the tipi. I followed inside, flinging blankets on top of what I hoped was Paron. He had been trained to lie still, and nothing moved under the covers.

The warrior—very tall, huge and brash the way young warriors always are—paid no attention to my hammer-swings, the butt of my gun crashing into his shoulders. I had grabbed the shooting end first because it was standing inside the tent flap and I was in a hurry. But the butt had no effect, so I took the time to turn it around and tried to shoot.

Too late I realized I'd taken out the bullets earlier that evening, so that it wouldn't go off while I cleaned it. Time stopped for me then, the world tilting and sound rushing in like wind through grass. For a brief second the click of the gun sat dead in my ears and the warrior looked at me like he might laugh in disbelief. I thought then that maybe he would come for me after all and we could just fight like men. But instead, yelping, he backhanded me with a huge paw that sent me flying right on top of Paron.

Paron couldn't help squealing. And even though I stood up and heaved with all my might against the warrior, trying to wrap a thong around his throat to kill him, the warrior just reached around me with arms longer than I had ever seen and pulled Paron up and out of the covers like an erupting tooth.

"Paaa-Paaaaaaa," Paron mawed as the warrior dragged him out of the tent. His limbs clawed at the big brave.

I ran after him, but the brave had a horse. He threw Paron and himself up onto it and rode off.

There must have been a hundred of them that night. I grabbed a stray pony flailing around in the dust and took off after the warrior. But my cousin pounded after me and pulled me down. He wrestled me to the ground, said, "You will die that way too, Ouray. Let him go for now."

If I were a dying animal I would've shit then, let my urine go. It was as if I'd deflated right into the earth. I felt all I had were hip bones and stretched skin. I lay my head back and stopped fighting my cousin.

My cousin let go of me.

I turned away, licking dirt. In the dark I was past tears, past the fight. There was just the tilting feeling, and then a black pit opened up, yawning forever. I fought it with fury. But it kept getting bigger and emptier, that blackness, no matter how furious I became.

Humming. I hear humming. Closer and closer, drowned out now by my heart thumping. The pink flower skirts graze my teeth and all of a sudden I've got a hand on my skull.

"Hey!" she says, little girl voice. She keeps humming, touching what's left of my burial blanket, the buckskins I was wearing when I died. Her fingers leave my head and I can tell by the small amount of dirt coming down and hitting my cheekbones that she's inspecting the overhang above me.

Finally she sits beside me, exactly where Chipeta sat. "How come you're not all gone?" she asks.

Huh?

"I mean, I read in the library about this stuff. It doesn't take very long for a skeleton to disappear, unless you've got a nice dry place. But your place has some holes." She touches the folds of my blanket just a little. "Nice blanket. Nice buckskin. I was reading about buckskin too. How you make it the way the Indians—I mean, you—must have. Talk about a yucky process! Scraping off all that flesh, then tanning it with brains. The guy who wrote the book says you can use cow brains these days, but they turn bright pink in the blender."

Why does she know this stuff? I'm amazed. What's a blender?

"Anyway, here you are." She notes my beads, the gun. OURAY is etched in it, a gift from Kit Carson, that weasel. Married a Navajo and sold them for slaves at the same time. He served some purposes though.

"Ouray? *Chief* Ouray? Well I'll be horn-swoggled. My dad always says that. Horn-swoggled. Not sure what it means, but he says it when he's surprised."

I wait.

"Wow. Chief. Chief Ouray. Hail to the Chief! Nice to find you. You know, nobody knows where you are. We did a unit on you in school. You're a big local hero, you know that? So, should I keep you a secret?"

Lumps form in the place where my throat used to be. My head moves beneath her fingers, so slightly that she might think she did it herself.

She wipes her hand across her nose. Getting up, she gathers her skirts like the ladies used to do when I was alive and stands in front of me. Her fingers go on my head again and she squats down, eye to eye-socket.

She's a brown-haired kid, eyes sort of blue with yellow specks. They are nice, big eyes. Sad, though, in spite of her bounce. She puts her forehead to mine.

"Don't worry," she whispers. "I won't tell. Just as long as I can come back and we can talk. I'd like to have someone to talk to."

Okay. And in her skid down the slope that, even so, has a kind of grace to it, I catch a whiff of what Chipeta must have been like when she was very young.

Weaver

MADDY

I look at the back of Barbara in the newspaper photo of the medics hoisting Trent on board the helicopter bound for Galveston. That lovely strawberry blonde hair. Still longish, still curly. I've got the Ouray arrowhead in my hand again and I really should put the newspaper in the trash. It's weeks old by now. But today I have to get ready to go to Mesa Verde for a seniors' visit of the new exhibit, and I am behind schedule. Mildred will be by at any minute. I lay the arrowhead back on the table, finish my morning coffee in the rose teacup my mother left me, and take it to the sink. Put on my gloves, coat, hat. Look one last time down at the photo. My old hands reach out as if to touch Barbara's hair, just the way I did when I taught her Sunday School when she was a little girl. That was before her father died and she and her mother left La Plata for a while. Interesting how Barbara came back to this place. And how she grew up to marry and become a weaver, and face, now, a whole other sorrow…

BARBARA

When Trent fell in—my firstborn, my gifted son—I lost all interest. But now—I'm faced with weavers from the prehistoric past who knew so much. Nets made of human hair, rabbit fur cloaks, a whole museum of this. Right now I've got my fingers tapping the edges of a blanket of turkey feathers and yucca, the former for weft, the latter for warp. The blanket comes from a Basket Maker burial, wrapping a mummy sequestered 2,000 years ago in a cave nearby. It's dark brown, with white, down-feather zigzags and—most exquisite of all—small touches of bluebird feathers. I rub the fabric delicately between my fingers, feeling in each of my hands, in every fluid cell and throbbing muscle of them, the itch to weave again. I sigh. I am so glad of this. After Trent's accident, I sat paralyzed, and the desire in my fingers to knit and weave and dye willow bark died too. It was as if my weaving had rotted and torn and fallen off, never to be finished again. I would wake up nights, sweating from dreams of rugs on clotheslines forever receding into the distance, or baskets thrown in boiling water, so hot they disintegrated. Sweaters unraveled into ghost towns, stray threads on wind.

I have knitted and woven since I was eight or nine. When I went to college I majored in art and ended up hip-deep in yarn, willow stays, dyes of indigo and cedar. I thought I might turn into a Painter, with a capital P. Wasn't that what happened to art majors? Or at least a Sculptor. But I kept knitting and weaving, and my art evolved out of that.

The blanket and I are in the basement of the museum at Mesa Verde National Park. I remember coming here as a kid, putting my hand to the glass of the displays upstairs, awed at the water jars and yucca sandals and space-coiled winnowing baskets. I went home from those visits and peeled yucca apart, tried to weave from moist green stems. But it never worked, and it took me years to learn that yucca stalks have to be soaked first, soaked and teased apart, and woven wet across the knee.

So I am back at the Park of my childhood. Back on a grant to come two days a week to the basement and study textiles. The Park Service hopes I'll be able to weave replicas from my time here.

I landed the grant two months before Trent's accident. I remember how pleased I was, how light and autumnal that day seemed after hours spent hovering over blankets and cloaks and baskets that hadn't been touched in years. The leaves were changing, the slopes of the peaks on fire with aspen going gold. September, late September, and I used my newfound clout with the Park to take my family camping along the canyon rims, to places not accessible to the general public. We spent several weekends that autumn putting our sleeping bags on the ground like spokes of a wheel, so that each of our heads lay in the center and our bodies radiated toward the trees. There, hair touching, the soapy scent of my two sons and the slightly sweaty smell of my husband reaching me, we watched the sky. The cool dirt would lie firm under our hips and shoulder blades, and we would stare at the great winking Milky Way.

I remember how we talked in quiet tones of sparse conversation on those trips. Trent—always just Trent, his dad somehow pleased with Trent Sr., instead of labeling his son a "junior"—might ask why Mars was red, or Brandon whether the moon really was made of cheese the way Todd Lemmon at school swore it was. Trent Sr. might see a meteor, and he would hold my hand, an extra strut extending between two of the spokes. In the dark I might even tremble, still, if my mood was right, with the food put away and no worries creasing my mind like horsetail clouds. After ten years I still loved the feel of his coarse male hair topping his fingers, knowing how black and curly it was, aware as one is aware of an imprint how big and callused and well used his hands were, what they felt like on my hips in the middle of the night, how they squeezed differently when needy as opposed to horny or tired. Sometimes it scared me, that this man loved me, that I was somehow willowy and calm enough to receive him.

The coarse hair of my husband's hand reminded me of the horse hair the Utes cut to make handles for their water ollas—big jugs made of squawbush coiled very tightly and covered with pine gum to seal them. The horse hair, twisted, looped in a small rope for handles, adorned each side of an olla like a set of ears, and for decoration they left a bristle of it, like the brush from a man's shaving kit, sticking out on either side of each ear. It was this bristle that carried the same texture as the whorls on my husband's hands; the only difference was how curly Trent Sr.'s were and how straight the hair from the horse. I loved both, finding something so humorous in the horse hair, so masculine in Trent Sr.'s. I wondered if Ute women laughed at their horsehair fringe, or thought of their husbands as they tied it on.

My family, the one I had safe and sound just weeks ago, would fall asleep watching those stars. Fall asleep atop rock formations whose cliffs below were full of the ruins of the Anasazi. Fall asleep knowing they would wake up, unchanged. *The religious beliefs of the Indian cultures are based on natural events, animals, and the relationship of people to the earth.* I drifted into dreamtime with sayings like that, cut whole-cloth from museum plaques, dioramas, films, what-have-you. Once, I swore I woke up nuzzled by a bear, but in the morning I could not tell if it had been Trent Sr. instead. It didn't matter, really; what mattered was a lingering animal heat, a fluidity to my limbs, the way in which flipping pancakes for my children in the morning brought such an odd mingling of maternal and sexual delight. I remember putting my nose to my oldest son's hair then, bending over as he ate flapjacks and inhaling, my arm around his chest until he protested.

There's a pang, and the turkey feather blanket with the bluebird feathers falls from my hands. Hair. He has none now.

SARAH

Snarling to myself like Beowulf snapping at flies. You won't get to me. *Hair pulled back so I can't lift my head up.* You won't get to me. *My teeth cut into each other, upper line sealed to lower line with my jaw clenching. It clenches so hard it hurts. When I was six I thought I'd die of tetanus. Lockjaw. Not speaking, not screaming. It didn't matter how many shots I had when I was a baby. Now I'm ten and a half, and I'm afraid of fire.*

You won't get to me. While a white lab coat...a white lab coat with— Choking noise. Choke it back. Burning. *Float to the ceiling.* Light fixture. See everything the way a crow sees things. *Numb. Numb the fire. Crawl out of your skin. Nothing but a bag of bones. Sack of skin. Heart shrinking to nothing as rubber fin—fin—fing—*

Shrapnel. A Walter Cronkite word on the six o'clock news. Napalm. Wounded men from Viet Nam. Torn up by shrapnel. Dumping napalm.

Napalm. Fire. I am not here. *She is not here.* Shrapnel. Slivers. Shreds. Splitting. S-words. *She's ripped bits of S-words as she closes out the pain. How could—? How could—? Like being operated on while she's still awake. Like rats, pawing and tickling and gnawing and— Ugncgh. Either that or the bruising feeling.* I am not here.

Shreds. Slivers. Slivers of glass. What's left—slivers of glass. Sliver for Indians, a big one, the Utes and Anasazi and Spider Woman. Another one for all the books, for Little House *and* Nancy Drew *and Mozart when he was five. One for the snow geese, the peaks, the beautiful peaks with aspen—go there go there—I can't—One now for Trent, the Fire Boy.*

Napalm. I've left. Crow on the ceiling. *She's unconscious. Both of us.* Both of us: *Help me.* Way down inside. Screaming.

Shrapnel. S-words. It's done now. For another time. The napalm dies back. The men come out of the jungle on the news. My jaw won't unclench. *She*—I have made it again. My jaw says: *you won't get to me.* It wants to burn the house down.

BARBARA

Paleo-Indian through Archaic through Basket Maker through Anasazi. On into Navajo and Ute, and then, in 1776, the Spanish of Escalante's expedition. The eras of Mesa Verde. Textiles of the American Southwest. I'm adjusting a Navajo sash, on loan from Hubbell Trading Post, when I hear my name.

I turn from the exhibit, the one I will be enhancing with replicas, the one which justifies my grant money. It's late December now and the museum is a cozy place, what with Christmas decorations mixed with Indian exhibits and the musty smell of old walls. Christmas is something I loathe this year, but here is the one place I can almost enjoy it.

I brighten when I see the source of the name-calling. "Mrs. Oodegaard!"

She stands there looking almost shy. "Gracious, Barbara, I was your Sunday School teacher decades ago. Call me by my first name."

I blush. "Sorry."

The museum echoes with old people. Lavender, roses, lilac scents, the tap here and there of a cane, an old man clicking his teeth as he stares at the panel next to mine. "We're not open yet," I say, noting how proprietary I've become. *We're* not open. "How come—"

Maddy puts a soft hand on my arm and chuckles. "It pays to be old. The Fifty-Five Plus Center wrangled us a free tour of the new exhibit. Provided we didn't mind the fact that it's in progress. I imagine they think it's akin to seeing a dress rehearsal."

"Oh," I say. Now I am suddenly shy.

"I've been meaning to call you. Frankly, I'm happy to run into you here. I have no more excuses this way."

"Excuses? To call me?" I fish in Maddy's eyes. This must be about Trent.

She speaks before I can ask. "I am so sorry, Barbara."

Her hand stays light on my arm. I turn to my exhibit case and watch it grow fuzzy with tears. *We're* not open yet. As if I belonged here. As if this opportunity, this grant, this job, wasn't all going to be over in a month or two. As if my little boy wasn't going to come home someone so different. I have been to Galveston. I know what's in store. A month or more and he's home. I tuck the sash around the mannequin of a Navajo medicine man, and falter back into Maddy.

I feel a motherly squeeze, an arm around my shoulders. The arm is plump, smells of old lady. My arm is bird-like, weak. I let myself be comforted just a bit, just enough, just as I used to at age six, when Bobby Mason kicked me in the church rec room, and I went crying to Maddy for help.

Back in my room. *Help me.* The upstairs room. Away from his hateful face, that camera he sometimes uses that goes flash like lightning, that same camera that can take such pretty pictures of canyons and prickly pear. *How can that be?* Dark now, and I'm Shrapnel Girl again. If I can see a deer, sometimes some of the pieces of myself glue back together. The yard light's off tonight but the moon is full and the side lawn is glowing and snowy.

My heart dies. No deer.

But wait. What's beyond the yard? A light, not moonlight. Oodegaard's window, square, filmy from curtains. Maybe a shadow behind it. *Can she see me?*

I pull back. Think about a dead man hanging in the basement. I don't mind bones, like the skeleton I just found, Ouray, or like those skulls at Mesa Verde. But rotting flesh, that's a different thing.

I slip down into the bed, not safe, and lie there for a long time. Not breathing. *What if Oodegaard saw me? What would she see? What would she see? Lab coat sandpaper chin fingers—*

But I don't even want to know what she'd see. Creepy old lady anyway, white and fat and a dead man in her basement. I can just hear Ricky sneering, *He hung himself five years ago, stupid. His body's not there anymore.*

But it is. I can feel it.

I sweat under the covers. I listen for the heater, strange noises, my body stiff until I think about being too tired for school. So I shove Oodegaard and her dead husband and Ouray and Mesa Verde all out of the way. I drift off.

A thud at the window wakes me up. My heart gobs in my mouth just like with the lab coat basement thing. Was there really a thud? God, it was right above my head. Curtains and the window. Maybe I can see a shadow like I did Oodegaard, and sure enough—I suck in my breath and peek upward—there's a bird-shadow, a beak and oval body. I stand on my knees and slowly lift the curtain.

A goose sits on the sill, white as the moon. Its eye looks in at me, right at me. My mouth hangs open. Everything is yellow and white and downy, like Clara's dress in the Nutcracker. The snow, the bird, the moon. All white and golden except for the eye. The black, round eye.

There's nothing like an eye boring into me. *I'm being seen.* Burns right to *down there.* Down there all red and shrapnel and—

Don't see me don't see me. Please *don't see me.*

But the bird cocks its head like it's surprised. Like it's saying, No? You don't want me here?

It's too beautiful and kind, that goose. I trip up on tears, choke. *Not meant for me, not.* I fall back down to my pillow, bite it to stop crying.

To hell with the goose. To hell to hell to hell.

I hear a flap of wings. Too late, I realize I need to ask it something. Too late, I want to know, *What are you doing here?*

Lessons

SARAH

Me and Ricky have piano on Wednesday afternoons. Instead of taking the bus home, we walk through a very boring, newer neighborhood, to our piano teacher's house. No matter where we live we have to take piano lessons. Mom makes us because she thinks music is important. Not just any music, but classical. All we have in our house are records and records of classical. I hear there's other kinds. Some of the girls at school like country-western, and Ricky somehow found out about ragtime. At the Kittredge Hotel, too, they do blues and folk music. But we never learn any of that, and Mom always finds teachers I hate. They usually have big moles on their foreheads or prissy lips. This time we have a lady with hair that doesn't move. Mom picks us up at four.

The neighborhood is next to the school, which sits on a mesa above town. If you look down you can see the old, main part of La Plata; if you look up to where the sun goes down you see the peaks. It's a great view but the houses up here are all aluminum siding and single stories with square lawns and station wagons in the driveways. I hate them. At least our house looks sort of like a log cabin, and doesn't have that siding. Our piano teacher's house is just as bad as all the others around it, and it's so neat inside I wonder how anybody can play real music in there. A wrong note and the drapes might tear.

If I have to learn music, I'd rather hang out with the bum down at the rail yard, the one at the roundhouse I'm sure our bus driver knows. Our bus driver's an engineer in the summer for the narrow-gauge train that runs for all the tourists. But even in winter when the train doesn't run, which is now, I'll see the bum at the rail yard on warmer afternoons, strumming a beat-up guitar through gloves with the fingertips cut off. The gloves remind me and Ricky of Oliver Twist.

"Please suh, can I have some music?" Ricky will imitate, holding out his hands toward the bum from far away so the bum won't see him. I always laugh at Ricky when he imitates because he imitates perfectly. Mom says he has a good ear.

I've never seen the bum with sheet music; he just seems to know songs by heart. I want to ask him how he does that, staring at him on Saturday while Mom goes into Safeway across the street. He's messy—I'm always accused of being messy. And he's got a funny hunter's hat sitting lopsided on his head, dingy overalls, hands that even from a ways off I can see are hands that work. They build stuff, use grease, clean trains. This morning he swallows coffee from a chipped mug, but once I saw him swig from a flask he pulled out of his coat pocket.

What you see is what you get; "No bones about him," Mom says, back from the store to catch me gazing at him. But Mom's voice has that snap to it; she ends her sentence too short. I throw her a secret, disgusted look but it just makes me sink again inside. *No help from her.* She hates being here, you can tell. Hates the West it seems to me. Listening to her, you'd think the only thing that mattered was how many college degrees you had and what kind of books you read. She's from Back East. She doesn't seem to think the peaks matter, or the hillside behind our house, or Mesa Verde or the train with its yellow cars and big black engine and coal smoke and whistle. At least Dad likes to be here, in the Rockies. At least he appreciates camping and rocks and doesn't make fun of other people who don't have degrees.

I look back at my bum with no bones about him. The bum's got working hands and can play music by heart and he looks like he's lived here all his life. I'm sure he never went to college.

I turn and follow Mom back to the car. *You got too many bones, Mom.* I glare that thought into her back.

I have my lesson first while Ricky waits in the living room, daring to put his soiled homework on Mrs. Iverson's glass coffee table. Iverson's hair never moves; every strand seems welded to the next. I have a hard time concentrating, thinking that her hair looks like a blonde version of those helmets the soldiers over in Viet Nam wear. There is something really wrong with hair like that.

My half-hour lesson is horrible. It's like being in church and wanting to laugh out loud at some dippy hymn. I want to swat the blonde helmet and make it roll on the carpet like a Barbie-doll head and run away. I'd go straight to the bum and tell him all about it, and I'm sure we would die laughing. Besides, today there's another thing making me itchy; I've got some other plans.

Mrs. Iverson seems as relieved as me when the lesson finally ends. I'm supposed to be proud of the fact that I'm advanced enough for Chopin's etudes, but the truth is they bore me to death and I think they're too hard. Besides, Ricky's by far the better piano player. He hears music as exactly as he hears how other people talk, and he's got bigger hands. So I whisper to him as we cross paths after I'm done that I'm going to visit a friend down the block while he has his lesson.

I've never done anything like this before. It's kind of scary because what if Ricky gets mad? I hate him being mad all the time. But at first he just looks puzzled and scowls out from under his eyebrows.

"Go on, Ricky," I say, "I'll be back by four. I promise." And I tap my wrist, where my new watch that I got for Christmas sits.

"Okay." He doesn't look too happy at being left alone with Iverson.

"Sorry," I say, and leave before he can say anything else.

Outside, I take out my present, all wrapped up, and a piece of paper. On the paper is an address. Trent MacIntosh, Sr., 1115 Aspenridge Road. Or so the phone book said this morning when I looked it up.

I couldn't believe my luck. Not only was his name the same as his son's (how many Trent MacIntoshes could there be in La Plata?), but the address meant the house was in the same block as Iverson's. The paper said he was home now, and I came up with an idea instantly. I grabbed a coloring book I never used and wrapped it up in birthday paper. I put it next to my music book and caught the bus wondering how I would ever get through the day until I could see Trent.

I have to say I'm a little disappointed that he lives in this neighborhood; it's not a neighborhood that likes things not perfect. Poor guy, coming home all swathed, his body evidence of one big screwup. But it's not his fault, and it's not his fault he lives in this neighborhood either. Kids can't help where their parents send them.

The MacIntosh house, though, has a shaggy lawn peeking through patches of snow. There are leaves that have never been raked up from last fall. "WELCOME HOME, TRENT" looms on a banner over the big living room window. For the first time, I get nervous. Not just nervous-excited—I've been that way all day—but also nervous-afraid. I make a fist to knock on the hard wood of the door. My fist hangs there in the air a minute. I feel my guts loosen and to stop that more than anything I go ahead and knock.

Footsteps. Pad pad pad. They must have carpet. Click of a lock, groan of the door opening.

"May I help you?"

I can't say a thing. I stand there like an idiot with my eyes bugged out. A nice-looking blonde woman—the woman whose back I saw in the newspaper—waits in the doorway, looking down at me.

"I… I, um…"

The blonde woman spies the present. "Oh, honey, is that for Trent? Are you a classmate of Trent's? I'm so glad. Not many people have visited—" Her voice trips up, and cloud-shadows drift over her eyes. "Oh, come on in, honey. What's your name?"

"Sarah. Sarah, um, Graves."

I pad after her on the squishy carpet, a huge lump coming into my throat out of nowhere. Mrs. MacIntosh's sweater slips off her shoulder. Sloppy and cool-looking. Mom's sweaters all have closed necks. And Mrs. MacIntosh walks so, I dunno, easily. Not all rigid and with her head eight miles in the air. She's like a big bowl of beef stew on a very cold day. My mouth fills with spit and tears. My tongue goes fat and numb because I didn't expect to feel like this. I didn't expect to feel any of the things I'm feeling.

Mrs. MacIntosh takes my hand into the kitchen.

"You can see Trent in a minute. But you look cold, so maybe you'd like some cocoa first?"

Mrs. MacIntosh peers at me.

I nod yes for an answer. Now my mouth's dry. *What does she see?*

Mrs. MacIntosh smiles. "I thought so," and turns her back to the stove while my chest constricts and my mouth goes between dry and wet and I remember the sweater so that when I'm older I can learn to wear them off like that, all warm and sloppy and safe and easy, long fingers putting a hot cup of cocoa in my hands.

The first thing I notice about Trent's room is his bed. It takes up most of it, and seems to be one enormous piece of wood carved in the shape of a sleigh.

"Wow," I say, staring at it.

Mrs. MacIntosh smiles. "Trent's dad made it. He's a furniture maker."

"Wow."

"I'll leave you two alone." She pats my shoulder and leaves the room.

I turn to Trent. I'm glad his mom left before she found out that me and Trent have never met before. Most of him is under covers, but his face is out and only the right side has real scar tissue. I guess I'm relieved that he doesn't look as horrible as all those pictures in the paper.

"Hi," I say. "You—um—don't know me, but—um—I wanted to meet you."

"Why?" Trent's voice rasps and it sounds as if he's short of breath.

"Can you talk okay? My name's Sarah."

Trent nods slightly. "Just my lungs—I guess they fill with fluid after stuff like what happened to me, but it's getting a little better."

"I'm sorry about what happened."

"Me too."

It's all awkward and silent. I look around the room. Beside the bed is a plain chest of drawers and some NFL posters on the wall. "Get Well" signs from his class plaster the area around the dresser.

"Has anybody else come to see you?" I ask.

"Not since I first got home. And even then, not too many."

"I bet they're scared."

"How come you're not?"

The tears I fought back with his mom come up in my eyes again. *What is this?* Usually I'm so good at pretending to be normal and happy. Usually I don't even think I have tears. "'Cause," I say. "I'm just not." I put on my Stubborn Face.

"Oh."

I wait to see if Trent will say anything else.

"Well. I brought you a present." I pull out the wrapped gift.

"Thanks," he says. "Will you open it for me?"

I waver, midway through handing it to him.

"Can't you open it?"

Trent pulls his hands out from under the sheets. The fingers are wrapped in a weird splint thing made of plastic and gauze, both hands held in place by it. Underneath the gauze, I can see the skin trying to pull in the opposite direction from the splint. The skin wants to contract his hands back into a permanent curl but the splint won't let it. The skin itself is warped and swirled and discolored.

Knives stab my gut and my Stubborn Face crumbles. *He can't draw. Stupid, stupid me. Why didn't I know that? I read the papers I could have figured it out It's always my fault I always mess up*

Dissolve dissolve disappear

Somebody lets out a huge sob, and the coloring book falls to the floor.

"Sarah, honey, what's wrong?"

Mrs. MacIntosh there in a flash, arms wrapping around me. Trent crying too, shrieking, "It's my hands, Mom! I know it's my hands! I'm a freak, Mom!"

I shake my head hard through the tears. I wipe my nose on the sleeve of my sweater while Trent's mom moves me closer to Trent's bed.

"Trent, honey, Sarah's saying it isn't your hands." Trent's mom sits on the bed and places a palm on Trent's forehead. Trent is crying almost as hard as me. I can't stand that I've hurt him so much. I stand crooked in Mrs. MacIntosh's free arm. Mrs. MacIntosh rocks both of us a little, letting us cry.

Finally, when we stop crying so much, she turns to me. "What was that all about, honey?"

I sniffle. Too hard to explain, everything's a jumble inside. I'd run but she's got her arm around me and she doesn't seem mad and—and—"I just—just wanted to give him a coloring book," I say. "But I didn't think about his hands and—and—and I messed up again!" I start wailing once more.

"Shhhh. How did you mess up?"

"Stupid, stupid of me. He can't draw! So I gave him the wrong present!"

Trent stares at me. *God I'll never come here again I swear.* Trent's mom keeps rocking me though, breathing into my hair. "Shhhh. It's okay. It's the thought that counts," she says.

"They all say that."

A sneer. A Ricky sneer. Mrs. MacIntosh pulls back and looks at me. "Sarah, honey, where'd you get so cynical?"

"Huh?"

"Never mind. Look, no one has come to see Trent for a long time.

All of the other kids stay away. The mayor came his first day back, and that's been it. People care, but I think this scares them. You have a lot more courage than most of them. Your visit means everything."

I dare to look up, finally, at Mrs. MacIntosh. "Really?"

Tears swim in her eyes the way I know they are in mine. Why? Why is she crying too? Mom never cries over me.

"Yeah," says Trent from the bed. We both turn to look at him. You'd think we'd forgotten all about him. We stare at him like deer do, discovering someone in the same clump of juniper. Trent actually chuckles. Soon we all start to laugh a little, me still sniffling and not knowing if I am the biggest idiot that ever lived, or if maybe I've found a new friend after all.

BARBARA

Sarah is the second white-winged creature besides me that my son has seen since coming home. She went as fast as she came though, muttering something about a piano lesson, and now I watch Trent resting in the sudden stillness of his room. I hang off in the hallway. He's listening, I think. *Listening to what?* Don't know. His own heartbeat, maybe. The small flutter of breath against pillow. The miracle of his existence in this little room with the Colorado light forming a rectangle on his hands, on his face. He stretches his arms into it like a cat so that I know that the warmth of it must be like love, the same as love. He must marvel that something warm can feel good to him now.

He told me, two days ago, how snow geese came to him in his dreams in Galveston. Huge flocks of them. There was the light touch of feathers, whiffles, whispers. White wingstrokes on his seared skin. They came just in time.

He told me how he had moments of falling into a well of no hope, usually the culmination of hours of spiraling downward, brought on by pain or the hideous appearance of his fingers or the fact that he could not move. And then he would find himself there: a senseless country, like the cave his dad took him to once and then turned off the flashlight. The total darkness, the complete silence, were terrifying. When they got out into the light again, his dad told him and his brother how they used to torture people that way. Sensory deprivation, he called it. It could drive a man crazy.

I said I would speak to his dad about telling his boys horror stories like that, but he reached out to me and said no. He said it was good his dad told him that because it helped him to know what was happening to him. How his well of no hope was like that. How it was that dark. How it was very, very deep. But instead of bottomless silence like in the cave, there was a black despair, and that had sound. It was a wailing noise, a deep howl, like a mad coyote. And just when he couldn't stand anything anymore, couldn't stand to maintain bravery, or the last shred of faith, the sobs would release and the geese would come flying.

What are you doing here? What are you doing here?

He told me he asked them that. Asked the geese. He told me they fluttered over his eyes, stroked his skin like cool water on a sunburn, cushioned his throbbing head, nested at his feet. His first instinct was to fight them, to fight anything that touched his seared skin. But the geese didn't work that way. They clucked and caressed.

Goddammit goddammit goddammit. I know what you're doing here, he told me he said to them.

And then he told me, *They wanted me to live, Mom.*

His dad wiped his nose after those bouts of sobbing. Countless times he wiped his nose, Trent Sr. said to me at night in bed where Trent could not hear. He would come in and see the tears and snot streaming out of his son's face and take a tissue and wipe everything away.

"Oh, Trent, oh, Trent," Trent Sr. would say.

Hospital white. The Galveston paper. Trent Sr. in an endless vigil. Cards and flowers and presents from me, who stayed home with

Brandon, weaving and driving to Mesa Verde, until Trent Sr.'s mother could come now and then to stay with Brandon, and I could fly south. I was like one of the geese, my son told me. Blonde, light, soft, huge eyes, hands that knitted hundreds of sweaters. I was someone who made soft things to protect the body. I gave him a different kind of hope than his dad. After all, I was a girl, he told me, and didn't turn away at the sight of him.

Now, watching him cat-stretch, I am amazed that he hasn't tucked his hands away in disgust. He ponders them, holds them up to the light. Where before they were nothing but ghastly to him—and he would jerk them out of his sight—he now seems to find them fascinating. Maybe ugly, certainly warped, yes. There are promises of operations, plastic surgery, later on, which might improve things. Trent looks forward to that, he says. But for now, well, it must be because Sarah was all right with them. A pretty little girl his own age didn't run away from him. And because of that, something has transformed with no surgery at all.

I watch as he closes his eyes. Does he dream of Sarah? Perhaps he does. Only strangely, I think, if he does, it is because he is pulling her out of an abyss, and not the other way around.

There is a low clucking that moves like a wave through the geese in the field by the river.

SARAH

Plink. Plunk. I finger the piano at home. The piano sits in the den, which is the only room in the basement that's carpeted and finished. The TV is there too; Ricky and me watch re-runs—*I Love Lucy, Green Acres*—and the Viet Nam War on the news. We only get three channels and two of them are fuzzy. Outside the den door, there's the place where the stairs and the furnace and the open area into the garage meet. I avoid the garage. The only room down there that feels at all safe is the den.

I hated going from Trent's house. Late January and the snow was starting to fly again. I sat silently in the back seat and drew in the inside cover of my notebook. I drew the Four Corners. I labeled the Arizona one Trent. Because he was burned, like the desert. For Utah I put Ouray with a question mark. Utah was an old-fashioned way of saying Ute, but I didn't know just what kind of relationship was possible with a skeleton.

I'd just finished the Utah question mark when Ricky spilled the beans. Told Mom how I'd left Iverson's.

"Where'd you go, Sarah? It's dangerous for little girls—"

"I was visiting the boy who got burned. I gave him a present." I stuck my tongue out at Ricky. Ricky gaped at me.

"That was nice of you. What inspired that?"

"Oh nothing," I muttered.

"I can't *believe* you did that," Ricky said.

"Shut up."

The red beds hurtled past on one side, the river on the other. Mom took the old highway because the new one's too scary for her, but even then it seemed like we were leaving Trent's way too fast.

I wanted nice ladies in sloppy sweaters with hot cocoa. I wanted a bed like Trent's. I wanted to be able to play music like the bum and not have anyone tell me that was wrong.

Plink. Plunk. I remember the feel of Mrs. MacIntosh's arms.

Plink. Plunk. The piano starts up at the Kittredge Hotel Saloon downtown. My guitar man accompanies it. It's blues piano, played by ear. A whiff of it floats to the river, and on updrafts of cold air, sails into the den. My eardrum echoes. My heart leaps with joy for about half a second. Music.

But I shut it down as fast as it comes. *NO. YOU HAVE TO LIVE WITH THESE PEOPLE FOR A LONG TIME. NO.* If I feel any more joy, or motherly arms, I will not be able to bear it.

I play a scale but I wish I could play the blues. I choke back tears. Upstairs, Dad clears his throat.

Haunts

Somebody opens a door to let the dog out and I catch the sound of a man's voice rattling. Must be Sarah's dad. I'm rattling myself tonight; there's a wind and my bones roll a little when it cuts into the crevice. It's more than the wind, though; there's a bigger rattling inside of me that the wind just makes worse. I don't know why this happens, much less why I have not passed on.

I was in this crazy frame of mind when I started haunting a long time ago. I haunted because I was mad. I was mad and I couldn't do anything. I couldn't pass on to the Spirit World, and I couldn't do anything in the living world either. I'd lost the living world anyway. I spent all my life walking a fine line soothing white people so we could keep what was ours. But in the end it didn't work. It didn't even work inside of me. When I was alive, I thought because I'd grown up with the Spanish down in Taos and then joined up with the Utes again later that I could walk in both worlds and meld them till they were okay with each other. Till everyone could smoke pipes and tell stories around winter campfires.

But in fact there were two of me, two Ourays. A Spanish Catholic and an Indian warrior. I wanted for them to hook up, but when the Meeker Massacre happened just before I died it was like a cleaver cutting the final joint between the two, and I saw how they had been hanging by thin threads of backstrap to begin with. How they'd never get together and the only reason I thought they would was because when the time came and the Utes needed someone who could talk with the whites, I was it.

Kit Carson always liked me. He relied on me. But talking with him in Taos on his hacienda porch, looking out over the Rio Grande cutting the Taos plain into jagged halves, I realize now that I always felt like an impostor. I never really understood until the Massacre why it had to be so complete when I went over to the Utes. Because talking with Kit I had one foot on his porch and the other out in the wild somewhere, hunting deer. You just couldn't get the two together, and it took me all my life to figure that out.

I told the medicine man that. Didn't want any white doctor by the end. The medicine man said maybe that's why my kidneys were in such bad shape, trying to hold too much together that wasn't meant to be held, trying to hold all that waste. I didn't know much about medicine and it didn't really matter because I died anyway. Died and got shunted up this valley. My people meant well, but I still got shunted. This isn't my homeland. Chipeta told me later that they couldn't get up to my homeland, north of here to the Uncompahgre, because there were too many white men and my people didn't want them finding out about me, about where Chief Ouray was buried. Maybe that's why I was mad; I wasn't buried right.

At any rate, I was homeless. Lost a child, lost a land. Lost everything, especially after Chipeta died in 1924 and no one stopped to visit me.

I'd been warned about what rage was like, felt some of it on and off ever since Paron was stolen. I even took herbs for it. But up in my crevice it multiplied. No herb could cure this monster, and the fact that I haven't gone on tells me it's still inside. I lie here and clench my fist bones and snap my teeth at night mice scurrying over my nose. But even they get away except for a tail now and then, and I'm left with all my sorrow and anger and not a thing to do with it. It makes you stupid. It makes you blind. And one day a long time ago it made me so stupid and blind I got up and whirled around. I whirled around and landed right in the middle of the mining camp of Philistine, and its bookkeeper named Lars.

The best times to haunt came when Lars walked to or from work, or sometimes after lunch, when he might take a walk through the pines nearby. Philistine mine made me sick—huge iron buffaloes ripping into the mountain itself, evil rotten-egg smells every time they blew something up, falling-down wooden chutes vomiting silver-colored rocks out of the mountain's belly. I'd never seen anything so disgusting and I hated Lars for putting up with it.

"Heathen," I'd spit from behind Douglas fir boughs.

Lars stopped walking. "What? Who's there?"

"Rapists. Digging holes in mountains where no hole should go."

I dropped a feather and some fringe on the ground, objects designed to appear out of nowhere. Lars bolted away from them like a terrified pony, eyes bulging to their whites and his legs twitching.

"Who are you?" he croaked.

I hadn't had this much fun in a long, long time. I picked up the fringe and tickled Lars' face with it. Lars stumbled, his arms batting wildly. "Stop it!" he shrieked. "Who are you?"

"Oodegaard?" A voice came from beyond the trees, toward the mine.

"Uh," Lars threw a look backward, his expression twisting.

"Lars? Mr. Kerr. I have some questions about the books, if I may."

If I may! Mr. Kerr himself, Philistine's silk-vest owner. I sneered. All those frilly jackets and shiny boots of Congress came back to me, only Kerr didn't even pretend to give a buffalo hide about anything unless it had to do with making money or pleasing himself. Which were often the same things. A growl juiced in my throat. Mr. Polite, had a little mustache that sat on his fat face like a caterpillar on a mushroom. Coyote. Wealth could give anyone a good sheen.

"Yes, yes. Fine. I'm coming." Lars doubly scared now, an Indian haunting him upslope and the boss beckoning down. My blood curdled like a river in floodtime, mad now at Lars for being so meek, so easily shaken, mad at Kerr for the whole mess of Philistine.

I dropped the fringe again so that it fell back at Lars' feet. Lars' mouth opened in a scream every muscle in his chest worked to stop. I couldn't help a cackle, could practically feel Lars' heart racing. I let him go, watching him bumble down the little deer path toward Kerr, but not before beating a drum very softly, just so, knowing that Lars would hear.

MADDY

I think the first "attack," as I call them, happened a couple of years into our marriage. It was right after Ted was born, and after we'd been in Colorado almost two years. I was pregnant with Walter and Lars had been working the books for about a month when he went through five solid days without sleep.

I have trouble talking about Lars' behavior even now. Here it is three a.m. and I'm not sleeping again myself. Tonight the basement light is off next door; no deer are in the spotlight either. My arms rest on the window sill, my head resting, in turn, on my arms. It's a quiet night, maybe even too quiet. The feeling of Lars slipping from me is here again. I wake up in the middle of the night, feeling him gone, and I panic. So I get up and riddle everything with memory.

After three days of no rest, Lars began to get delirious. His eyes blazed with such an intense cold fire that he reminded me of Ichabod Crane. He would not stop working, even when there was no more work to be done. He carved Ted beautiful wooden toys in the old Swedish style his father had taught him, making little Viking boats for a baby so landlocked he couldn't see past the first steep rise of the mountains. He kept the fire blazing all night long. He finished the books for the week two days early, which was a good thing because by day five I knew he'd kill himself if I couldn't find a way to get him to bed.

The camp had a doctor who came every Friday. I didn't want to go to him with Lars' trouble because I didn't really know what his trouble was. How do you explain to a doctor that your husband won't sleep for five days straight? What kind of illness is that? I was afraid he'd think I was crazy, or Lars was, and I couldn't get Lars to go anyway. I couldn't get him to do anything he didn't want to do in those five days. Besides, Kerr was notorious for letting people go if they got sick too often, and we couldn't afford that.

But I knew the doctor had morphine. Little vials of it, and a syringe. He used it to treat mining accidents, injuries sustained from beams of timber falling on a man's head, or the wily blasts of dynamite that might burn off a man's hand. It had been used with great success to manage pain during the Great War. Of course, some of the men were addicted to it as a result, but I was hardly concerned about that with Lars. I just wanted one shot to knock him flat out. I would explain his absence to Mr. Kerr later, though because Lars was ahead on the work I didn't think it would be much of a problem.

The doctor always dined, in an elaborate lunch, with Mr. Kerr. Fortunately it was summertime (how we were all going to survive the winter in tents was something I didn't want to think about), and they ate outside, away from the mess and noise of the mines, in a kind of gentleman's picnic.

As soon as the doctor was out of sight, I slipped inside the tent. The vials were right there. I grabbed what my hands could carry—three vials, and three syringes. I'd had a little nurse training back in Nebraska when the war was on and everyone was mobilizing. After that, too, I'd done some nursing when the flu epidemic hit and I lost my grandfather, two cousins, and an aunt. I'd learned to use a syringe once, and had watched doctors do it several times, so I thought I could manage. I took them with me and hid them among the dishes while making Lars' lunch. Ted was sleeping.

Lars came in. His eyes were so glazed they looked like ice ponds. He mumbled incoherently and could barely sit still enough to eat. Oh boy, I thought, this is going to be a challenge. I served him a big bowl of stew, hoping that the food would focus his attention long enough to get him still in one place. As soon as he sat down I turned my back to him and prepped the vial.

"Gonna eat?" he asked. "Sit down with me. Let me tell what happened today—I swear I heard an Indian. Saw some fringe, and a feather, too. Scared me half to death, but—"

I put a gentle hand on his forearm. If I didn't stop him now, he'd talk all afternoon. His speech was curiously rapid, and crisp as lettuce. I glanced at him. He ran a shaking hand through uncombed hair.

"Lars. If you don't sleep, you'll die."

He looked at me with pity, as if he hated to make me panic but there was nothing to panic about. He was captured by a wild spirit that kept him enthralled. He wasn't going to die, are you kidding? He was already in heaven. He'd told me as much the night before. Life was too good to go to sleep. He might miss something. Why, just today he heard an Indian, right? Lights were flashing, parades were happening. Couldn't I see that?

I plunged the needle into the vial, sucked out the morphine.

"Eat! Eat with me. What are you doing?"

"Shhh…" I hid the vial in the fold of my skirt in one hand and held a bowl of stew in the other. I sat next to him on the bench, putting my bowl down in front of me. I placed the stew hand on his forearm. He looked at me with a faint moment of lucidity that almost made me think I didn't have to go through with the morphine. But that lasted about two seconds. As soon as the ice ponds were back in his eyes, and before the spell of my touch was broken, I gripped his forearm tightly and drove the needle into his bicep with my other hand.

At first he looked at me in complete disbelief. Then he shrieked, standing up and spilling his stew. "Whaddareyou doing, Maddy? Whaddare you doing?" He swatted the place on his arm furiously, as if that might rid him of the evil drug. "How could you—?"

I had destroyed his dream, his heaven on earth. He slumped after a minute, the morphine and, probably, the shock of my actions cracking into his hysteria. I managed to get him to bed right before he passed out entirely, and the look he threw me before his eyes flickered shut was one of utter hatred.

I drift in and out, remembering Lars, remembering the pines above Philistine where I haunted him most of the time. The night's still rattling but in the last little while I have felt cradled. It's a strange feeling, as if Chipeta were back, stroking my forehead. I used to hunt around here a lot, and take the waters at the hot springs up the valley. Chipeta would wait there with the other women while my fellow warriors and me went looking for deer. I lost an arrowhead once near here, when my arrow nicked a deer and fell out. I never found it.

Arrowhead, why that? Umm, sleep. Oodegaard. *Mrs.* Oodegaard. Lars' wife. Why her?

I got so used to upsetting Lars that it about killed me when he showed up one day in the trees again, confident and whistling. He had been avoiding them for a while, so I couldn't figure out what he was doing. Wasn't he frightened anymore? Didn't he have work to do? Curiosity got me. I straightened my buckskin, re-tied a loose moccasin (Chipeta made them for me the year I died), and grabbed my drum and feathers from a cache in the granite scree above a small side shaft of the mine. Down in the trees, Lars meandered on a deer-path. He followed a tiny alpine rill up the narrowing bowl of the mountain. I made my move.

"How dare you?" I said, deadly. "Whose land do you think this is, anyway? Do you really think you can own the trees? The rocks?"

Lars stopped, but without fear. Instead, he looked curious, almost feverish. His eyes shone so much they looked wet. "Who's there?" he asked.

Usual question, but no terror and so no fun.

I tried the standard feather and fringe trick. Lars picked them up, twirling the feather, stroking the fringe.

"Are you a real Indian?" he asked. "My father always said be careful of Indians. He hated 'em. But I never did get to see a wild one. Are you a wild Indian?"

Great Spirit, the man was babbling like Two Birds, the savant from our band everybody went to for divinations. With Two Birds, though, at least a little bit of sense could be made from his diatribes about buffalo living up above timberline, his harangues on the uses of mouse hides. But here was Lars, going on about his father and referring to Indians as "wild ones."

I struggled to rip the fringe out of his hands and tickle him with it as I'd done before. But he held on like a petulant dog. My spirits sank. Couldn't I successfully terrify at least one white man? And underneath, there was another awareness: Lars was actually talking to me.

Time to play my trump card. Covered head to foot in buckskin, hair braided and held together with beaded ties, I revealed myself. *Please, let his father have terrified the living piss out of him about Indians.*

For a moment, Lars did stagger. His hand flew to his chest. "My God," he whispered, the fear flickering back. But just when I was flushing with victory, the fear disappeared and the intense curiosity resurfaced.

I felt naked as a Spanish hog parading through the plaza at Taos. "Satisfied at seeing a 'wild one'?" I sneered.

Lars tried to touch the fringe of my sleeve, but I jerked my arm away. I didn't want any white man touching me. "I'm not some zoo animal!"

"Zoos? Zoos are fun! How do you know about zoos?"

"I've been to Washington, you idiot. The president took me to the National Zoo. It's disgusting what you do with our brothers, caging them up like that. Someday they'll eat you alive, you know."

Lars stared, his mouth shut, the silence inflating by the second. And then he burst into laughter. He laughed so hard he clutched his stomach and had to sit down on a rock by the stream. The trees bounced his laughter off of their bark. "An Indian in Washington! At the zoo with the president! My God! It's too much." He shook his head, tears leaking out of his eyes.

If I didn't watch it, I was going to kill him. For a brief moment I actually considered it, fingering the knife at my waist. Nothing had gone as planned today; Lars was in some bizarre mood incapable of being destroyed. But the warrior in me nagged—kill a person because he got your goat for a few minutes? What kind of unmanly act is that? That kind of thing turns a warrior into a clown and the last thing I wanted was to be laughed off.

No, better to go for Kerr, who could put me in a wolfish mindset just by twiddling his mustache. But Kerr wasn't around. And Coyote was a big spirit to haunt. It depressed me to think I might not be up for it, up for Coyote. So I fled, fists shaking in rage, up the scree slope above the valley bottom. I looked back once. Lars looked like a wild scarecrow, let loose from whatever cornfield he was supposed to be watching, still laughing and reeling.

"Hey!" Lars looked up when he realized I was gone. "Where'd you go? Come back. Tell me a story!"

But I did not answer. My mouth went straight with anger. I did not answer, and left Lars there on the rock, alone with his childish, pathological wonder.

MADDY

Night. Two a.m. That hideous light on in the Graves' basement again. I saw little Sarah Graves' face yesterday, too. She was out on the side lawn, making snow angels next to the deer tracks. When she stood up, she saw me looking out the window. I smiled, but Sarah looked like she'd seen a ghost and ran away. Maybe she's heard about Lars hanging himself. When I was a little girl, I always knew every community horror story. It was part of being a child. But something hard and adult and too wary pesters Sarah. Like that war vet I took care of awhile in the late '40s. He jumped at everything. About killed me once, thinking I was a Jap. But he belonged to our church and eventually he lost some of his edge, though he never did seem quite lively again.

I wonder about Sarah. I wonder what goes on over there. I wonder if I will never outlive the truth of Lars' death. If that's what people will remember about me—that I was the widow of a man who killed himself, and therefore the cause of it somehow. I still bear that look from strangers, though it happens less often. And I have friends, good friends, who know better.

Lars went on and on about that Indian when we lived in Philistine. Ouray, he said, over and over; it was Chief Ouray. I kept trying to tell him Ouray'd been dead forty-some years. No, he said, he was around. Him, or his spirit, was around. I play with the arrowhead that always reminds me of Ouray again tonight. It's a lovely reddish agate, smooth and beautifully made. Only the very tip is missing. I worry it like a rosary, the way I've seen the old Mexican women do during the one or two funerals we went to in Spanish Flats, south of the smelter down toward New Mexico.

I worry it and worry it. The smoothness of the stone is soothing; it feels safe and dangerous all at once, which is, I suppose, how all weapons must feel. I think about giving it to Sarah, because the light in the basement makes me think she needs something like that.

I sigh, lulled even though for the first time I have the audacious thought that one of these nights, maybe in the spring when it gets a little warmer, I just might tromp over the Graves' lawn and peek in. See who else is awake at this godforsaken hour, and why. And I certainly intend to befriend that Graves girl. But for now, I just stroke the arrowhead; my eyes droop out of staring at their basement window, and back toward sleep.

Ruins

SARAH

Dad can be just like us, smiling and burping, when he's away from home. Away from Mom. As long as I have Ricky there on the road with him, I feel safe with Dad. Life comes into him once we're in the car out from under whatever home does to him. He took me and Ricky to Mesa Verde in the late summer, after we'd been in La Plata two months and I was already deciding that of all the pretty places I'd lived, this was my favorite. Mountains and desert. Four Corners again. National monuments everywhere, four-thousand-foot-high deserts or fourteen-thousand-foot-high mountains, a place for whatever your mood.

When I saw Mesa Verde I decided that my culture was even weirder, because Mesa Verde made sense. On Dad's topo map the Park looks sort of like a turkey made by tracing the outline of your hand, each finger a different mesa separated by steep canyons. It sits exactly on the border between the mountains and the desert plateau, so it isn't too cold for growing corn but it isn't too dry, either. The ranger on the tour of Cliff Palace said that the Indians lived on the Mesa for eight hundred years before leaving. Then they left and nobody knew why, and the ranger kept talking about it as if they'd failed.

But I was doing calculations in my head. I knew my family had come to America in 1634. They were Pilgrims. And I knew they got to California by 1930, where Dad was born. In between they whirled around Vermont, Illinois, Iowa, and Nebraska, and built farms that never seemed to work for very long.

How many years was that, 1634 to 1930?

Almost three hundred. Three hundred years for an entire continent. Eight hundred years on one dry mesa without irrigation or tractors.

Anasazi is the name given cliff dwellers, but Dan Talayseva, a Hopi employee at the Park, tells me they prefer the term Hisatsinom, or "ancient ancestor." Anasazi could mean "ancient enemy;" Anasazi is a Navajo word and the Navajo can't claim them as ancestors the way the Hopi, and many of the other Pueblo tribes, do. The man told me to read *Book of the Hopi*, and I've done so. It has triggered a rash of other reading.

I read a lot on lunch hour. Today I cradle myself against a wooden bench out on the back porch of the museum, eating a sandwich from one hand and holding a book open in the other. It's February and cold but I don't care. The basement gets musty and on the benches out back I can look down into the canyon. Now that Trent is home, I find I need to be outdoors quite a bit. The canyon's pretty, and if I move my head a little I can glimpse parts of Spruce Tree House ruin at the bottom.

Today it's sunny, post storm. The snow from the night before soaks into the sandstone and lines, delicately, the inner branches of trees. I love days like this—cold, so clear you'd think the air capable of snapping. If I weren't here, I would go skiing, cross-country over open meadows crisscrossed with elk tracks.

I open my thermos and steam curdles into the atmosphere. For a minute I blanch, thinking of Trent's manhole, of scalding. It takes me a minute to calm down.

I cup my hand around hot tea and sit up, trying to get back to the book in front of me. I maneuver it between my legs so that my thighs can hold down the pages while I sip the tea. I'm looking at Basket Maker artifacts taken from Grand Gulch, from Mancos Canyon, from inaccessible caves lining so many cracks and gullies around the

Four Corners. Pictures and pictures and pictures of loot. Burial bags, yucca sandals, baskets lined with pitch, baskets with lids, winnowing baskets, plaited basket bowls, woven medicine bags. Loot. Huh. So much of it back east, in the Smithsonian, at the Heye Foundation, or in the Museum of Natural History. Mummies, stripped of everything and contained like frogs in laboratory jars in basements all over New York.

What would a New Yorker want with a mummy from Cedar Mesa? *Bring it back here.*

A shadow falls over my book. "They should bring it back here."

I look up. The Hopi man, Mr. Talayseva, is gazing down at me. I close the book, feeling a little bit as if I've been caught looking at dirty pictures.

"Come on, Basket Lady," he says. "I will show you something." He gestures toward the canyon, and I stand up, slowly.

"Look," he says, after we've hiked to the bottom near the ruin, me coming up beside him and sticking my neck out to the small concavity where he points. "Here is the spring of our legends."

"Up top," and he reaches and parts the wintry branches of a vine covering the sandstone overhang, "we have this symbol, for Salavi, the old leader of the Badger Clan. When he died, he left this spruce next to the spring here as a sign." And sure enough, the spruce grows by the overhang, and the cliff face holds a pictograph of a holy man, on his side, dead, with a spruce tree coming out of the water next to his head.

After that, he takes me to the round underground kivas, roofless now, at Spruce Tree. The ruin is not fifty yards from the spring and he notes details so specific and lovingly recalled that I start to laugh. All those archeologists! Not *knowing*. And here's this Hopi man, explaining the entire ruin.

"Why do you trust me with this?" I ask him, following the neat baton of his hair, wrapped in red cloth, back up the canyon. He's a permanent law enforcement employee who talks to very few people.

And nobody in Cultural Resources seems aware of his knowledge.

Mr. Talayseva turns to me. "I see the way you look at our ancestors' baskets."

That's all he says. But it almost makes me cry.

SARAH

Me and Ricky and everybody visit Spruce Tree House again. This time it's cold and not too many people are around, but I don't care. I promised myself next time I came here I'd I go into one of the back rooms behind the kivas in the plaza. They seem so private.

I slide away through a keyhole doorway. The room smells like cold dust, not wet at all, a musty smell. The walls of this room I can tell have stood up for the most part because where they didn't the restoration people used this kind of pink cement to glue them back together. The cement looks like that stuff they clean your teeth with at the dentist's office. So I can see where the walls must've fallen by where the pink cement is, and in the back here the cement's only up in the high places where the walls meet the roof of the rock shelter. The front wall fell down more, though, but that's the wall with the door and it faces toward the plaza and the weather, so no wonder.

Nobody can find me in here. I can hear Ricky and Dad and Mom and my Aunt Marion farting around outside along with a few other people. They're supposed to give a ranger tour in a few minutes and Mom and Dad like to take people here when they come visiting. Aunt Marion lives by herself in Iowa most of the time but she does stained glass. Once I dreamt she ran off to L.A., where Dad's from, and became an artist. I told Mom that and she snorted. I think she thinks artists aren't moral or something.

In the back room I'm cozy and it's small. A couple of manos and metates lie along a wall, for people to try out. I pick up a mano and kneel in front of the metate. *Anasazi women probably spent a great deal of time grinding corn.* Blue corn, blue and red and yellow. Pretty corn. At school some Pueblo lady came and made this flat bread called piki out of blue corn she ground. She had a hot flat rock and poured this goop on it till it formed a thin layer. It peeled off like a fruit roll and didn't taste like much. Still, maybe I can pretend to grind like her. Let's see. I got a buckskin apron and a rabbit fur cloak because it's winter, and those funny fat leggings they wear, and moccasins. My hair's long; I don't like those dumb butterfly hairdos Hopi maidens had even though I guess that was supposed to make them more attractive. Maybe my hair's left long because I'm already married and have a little boy with black hair and a toy bow and arrow.

Rushka rushka. Back and forth, the mano grinding on the metate. I take a handful of seeds I found in a pod outside and put them in the metate. *Rushka rushka.* The seeds break down into tiny pieces. I squint closer. I can see little grains of sand in with the seed stuff. The Indians wore their teeth down eating sand with the corn. It's what you get for using rocks for grinding, I guess.

"Sarah!"

Crud. I gotta go. I brush the seed stuff off into the dust and put the mano back in the metate, just the way I found it. I stand up and actually straighten my jeans like they're an apron instead. When I walk outside into the light of the plaza I have to blink to adjust. It takes me a minute, not just because of the light, but because at first I see Anasazi mothers everywhere, grinding and chatting on the roofs of the kivas, on a sunny winter day.

The ranger is talking. He explains how the kivas are ceremonial structures, and how they might have evolved from pithouses. Pithouses are what the Anasazi lived in when they were still Basket Makers and didn't eat as much corn or beans or squash. They've put a roof back on one kiva here, but most of them don't have roofs on them anymore. When we're standing around above one kiva's rim, a stick tickles the floor. The ranger gets down in the kiva, lets go of the wooden ladder and bends down to pick up the stick. "Paho," he says, holding it up for us to see. "Prayer stick. Someone still comes up here at night and puts them in the kivas. We've even found them in Balcony House, which has a locked gate so the only way you can get in there at night is by using the old toe holds from the top of the canyon. It's pretty steep."

I stare at the paho. It's notched and a few feathers are stuck in it. I open my mouth to talk. "Wha—which Indians?"

The ranger shakes his head. "They're very secretive. But maybe Hopi. Or even Acoma or Zuni. They all claim ancestry here."

"But the Hopi are the closest, and they're still four hours away by car!"

The ranger smiles at me. "You know a lot, huh? Yeah, they are. But why would it be Navajo or Ute? They don't make prayer sticks, and the Anasazi were the ancestors of the modern Pueblo Indians, right?"

"Ri-ght," I say, trying to think. "But still. How do you know?"

He sighs. "We don't," he says. "To be honest."

"So it's just a guess."

"A guess, yes. They don't tell us much."

"Why not?"

The ranger fixes his Park Service tie and looks at everyone else. "Let me get out of here and you all can climb down the ladder," he says. Nobody else seems as interested in the paho as I am. When he climbs up most of the others, including Dad and Ricky, climb down. Mom doesn't like ladders so she and Aunt Marion talk away from the kiva pit. The ranger squats in front of me, taking off his Smoky Bear hat and running fingers through his hair. He seems almost upset.

"When we got here—whites, that is—we didn't treat Indians very well. Did you know that?"

"Well, yeah," I say. "I know it wasn't like a John Wayne movie. Is that what you mean?"

"I mean we killed them off, took their land, and when it came to their ruins and burials, we just pillaged them." He shifts in his squat, drawing a finger through the dust at his feet. "It's like this. How would you like your churches destroyed? Your great-grandmother's body taken out of her grave and her wedding ring and fine dress sold to a museum?"

I stare at him. "I wouldn't like that at all."

"Right. But from the Indian point of view, that's what we did. We destroyed who they were."

Shrapnel Girl knifes into me. Slivers of glass flying everywhere.

"What's the matter?" he asks.

I don't say anything.

He hands me the paho and I take it. I roll it between my fingers, making the feathers twirl.

"Did *not*," I decide, finally, watching it.

"Did not, what?"

"Did not destroy who they were. Otherwise, this paho wouldn't be here."

I hand it back to him. He takes it from me. As I go down the ladder into the kiva, I see him wondering at it. Holding the sliver of it up. Like a whisper in the dust.

OURAY

"Hey, Chief, you ever see a paho?"

She's back again, up in my crevice, sitting in the only place there is to sit, to the right of my skull on a small ledge where the crevice widens just enough.

Paho. A word from my past. Taos Pueblo. Yes, I've seen a few pahos.

"Do you know they still put them in the kivas at Mesa Verde? I went there this weekend and I learned that. *Somebody* comes up there and puts them in at night. Even in high-up places where they have to use the old toe holds and must just about fall down the cliff every single time. Now that's dedication."

Not since Chipeta came the last time has my heart danced quite like this. This is news, this is good, good news. If I could smile I would. I would show her my smile, too, this little girl in the dress full of flowers.

"The paho was cool," she says. "So I made my own. See?"

She sticks out her palm. On it, a smooth stick with notches cut in it and the blue feather of a pinon jay looped through a slit in the top. "Not sure what the notches are for. But I've made mine just to have something to feel, like those Catholics always do in the movies with those beads. Makes me feel safe."

Safe? What does she fear? She's got enough to eat, and a house and a family. What could she fear?

The tilting feeling I had when Paron was taken, and again when the Meeker Massacre happened, revisits me ever so slightly. It increases after she says goodbye and skips back down to her oak nest. It's February, Great Spirit. What is she doing out, alone, in February, with the snow piling up, or melting into mud on sunny days? Something's not right here. I've watched her father in the yard sometimes, puttering, raking leaves, whacking icicles off the eaves. Been so jealous of him having a son and a daughter, intact, unstolen. But something sneaks inside me now, a worm. Does he treat them right? Are Sarah and that little boy of his happy?

I hope so. I hope so. Or I'll kill the bastard for not knowing just what a thing he has.

SARAH

The best time the best time the best time... Me and Ricky go with him to Flagstaff to drop off rocks at NAU. We drive down all morning, stop to pee and get gas and let Beowulf take a poop outside Kayenta at an old rest stop. I love this rest stop. It's got a ruined hogan at the bottom of a huge sandstone cliff that bends and folds around into little alcoves. It's especially pretty now because it snowed a couple of inches last night and so all the red sand and red rocks and clumps of sage are lined with white. The storm's past now and the sky has the kind of blue to it that's so bright Mom's relatives from back east can never believe it. They always think Dad puts a filter on his camera lens when Mom sends them pictures of us under sky like that, but when they come out here and see that that's how it really is their mouths drop open.

The sandstone cliff has crisscross lines in it. Cross-bedding, Dad says. These cliffs used to be gigantic sand dunes and it always amazes me that things can change so much like that. While Beowulf sniffs around I look for heart-shaped rocks. I found one once like that in Canyonlands and tried to give it to Dad because I knew it was his heart. Canyonlands is where he especially likes to go with his students. But he just left my rock on a picnic table even though I told him it was his. I had to go back for it.

In Tuba City we stop for lunch. It's a little diner, the kind we always go to with Dad, usually after hiking or camping when we're all grubby from exercise and I feel the closest ever to being like one of his students. That's when it's really the best.

This diner is white and light and has three clocks on the wall, one for Arizona, one for the Navajo reservation, and one for Hopi land. They all say the same time now, but Dad explains in the summer things get screwed up in Arizona.

"Why?"

"Because Arizona doesn't go on Daylight Savings Time but the Navajo Reservation does."

"So what's that mean?"

"That in the summer Arizona and California are on the same time, but the Navajo Reservation part is on the same time as us in Colorado."

"There's a third clock," Ricky says. "It says Hopi."

Dad sighs. "That's because the Hopi Reservation—"

"Which is right in the middle of the Navajo Reservation," I say.

"Which is right in the middle of the Navajo Reservation, that's right," Dad says. "Just to the east of here. We went through it at Moenkopi. Anyway, the Hopis stay on the same time as the rest of

Arizona in the summer."

"So you mean there's this little square of land in the middle of the Navajo rez that stays on the same time as Arizona?" Ricky asks.

"That's right."

"That's dumb," Ricky says.

"You could think that, yes." Dad's voice sounds dry like dust, sort of neutral and sort of not. He explains things like this to us all the time. Mom never does. He's a good teacher; he likes to teach. But sometimes I think he thinks we ask boring questions. Like we're too young for his mind.

We order Navajo tacos. Beans and beef on top of a big old slab of fry bread, topped with lettuce, tomato, onions, salsa, sour cream. Yum. Even Mom likes Navajo tacos, but she wanted to stay home. She said she wanted to be by herself.

Dad has restaurant coffee, the kind that makes his breath smell bad. Ricky orders a root beer even though it's freezing outside. He does that so he can burp. When he burps Dad kind of laughs like he knows he's not supposed to but does anyway.

We brought in a water bottle to fill up, the liter size for hiking that's plastic with a wide top. Dad does his double-jointed jaw routine. "AWi-I-DE Mou-TH PO-O-LY BOT-tle," he says, holding it up and working his jaw really wide. It's the only time I don't see his jaw tight, except when he's with his students.

But Ricky does it even better. You can hear his jaw bones wobbling on one another with each syllable. He takes the bottle from Dad and they compete to see who's best. I just watch. I can't do the jaw thing at all.

The cafe echoes, sort of empty. It's the first of March and nobody's around. An old Navajo pair sits in the corner—she's got those thick velvet skirts on and a big turquoise necklace. The man's almost entirely in black. Outside you can see round hills of soft stuff, banded in all those crayon colors I'd have never heard of except that they're in the crayon box. Burnt sienna. Raw umber. And then roses and pinks and dusty purples and even black, like little coal seams. In the summer those hills bake in the heat with the rest of the Painted Desert and the road next to them shimmers. In the summer I wear shorts and we hike and then I feel like I could be one of those boys like Ike or Peter, one of those boys who can hike anywhere, who want to go with Dad where no other sign of people exists, who are big and beautiful and tan and on their way to becoming scientists like Dad.

We finish our tacos. Dad likes it out here. Almost likes us out here. Ricky burps again and I try the Wide Mouth Poly Bottle jaw routine. I don't do very well, and practice to myself in the back seat, where no one can see me. After a while I give up, and by the time we get to Flagstaff I'm singing to myself instead, *Joe Hill* and *Down in the Valley* and *You Are Lost And Gone Forever, Oh My Darlin' Sarah-tine.*

I don't want to share a bed with Ricky. We'd camp, but it's too cold. There's two double beds in the motel room, the Flagstaff Inn. I always hate this part, even camping. Dad *right there* and Ricky *right there* and even though I'm glad Ricky's here I still don't like sharing a bed with him. Too many boys, too close too close too close...

I watch Dad's chest rise and fall in the dusk of the motel room. What if more than his chest rises? What if his whole body gets up? But he wouldn't do that, would he? Not with Ricky so close and all of us away from home, away from home? He's always safer away from home. A train blows a long whistle, moving fast I can tell. The air outside the motel seems full of something big and black and heavy all of a sudden, like it's being pushed aside too fast for it to get out of the way. The whistle dies off into the long black night. Ricky's hogged all the covers. The curtains are heavy and block out a lot of light, but some gets in around the edges.

Ricky and Dad are definitely asleep. I'm a girl, the only girl. I can't burp and do Wide Mouth Poly Bottle like Ricky. I've got my pajamas on, half the bedspread. I huddle with my hands clasped between my thighs.

Cold. Still too cold. Another train goes by. What time is it? Rise and fall, rise and fall. I finally jerk some covers back for myself even though Ricky's bigger than me and has already learned from Dad—learned from Dad—rise and fall, rise and fall. Learned from Dad—what? Dad's Mr. Meek most of the time, but I know better. I know better, and it's because of this that I have to wait up nights, listening to trains and feeling just awful, and afraid.

Part Two

Earthsong

We haven't experienced burning the way the trees and the animals and all the live things do. Smoke, yes, from fires down below, and of course far back in our memory lies the pain of hot liquid states, the cocktail of magma we were before the gods allowed us to cool and we set into our current hard gray forms. You can see the scars if you look closely, the dikes of schists, the flecks of mica. But it has been a long time, though we know that the Earth's heart is made of fire, and so every heart upon it, having sprung from this interior, must be—can only be— also made of fire.

The snow geese tell us that on our forested slopes men dressed in drab green uniforms post notices with a strange looking bear on them that say: *Only You Can Prevent Forest Fires.* And within a day or so of lightning smoldering a tree, licking its hands around a dead stump, or infusing dry meadow grass with flame, these same green men know about it. They spend whole summers in watchtowers on promontories below us, just looking for smoke; if there are enough of them, we occasionally feel the tickle of their feet on our flanks. When a fire does happen, then, the two-leggeds come with flying machines which dump red sawdust and water all over the flames; they come with axes and masks to breathe through; they bring giant yellow dirt-moving machines and cut swaths through the forest so the fire finds nothing left to burn. The aftermath is a blackened, smoking landscape ringed by felled trees, ribbons of upheaved forests. And in the areas that didn't burn, the tinder builds. And builds and builds.

It's strange, because the brown two-leggeds used to deliberately set fires. We would see them crawling around the high meadows with torches each autumn after the elk had gone down to lower elevations. The brown *two-leggeds didn't try to control their fires much, but there didn't seem to be layers and layers to burn, either. It's hard to tell—the years go by quickly yet so slowly, our time measured not by their seasons necessarily but the combined effect of eons of seasons—yet from up here it seems to us that these burnings were routine, and between the brown-leggeds and the lightning, most of the forests and meadows found themselves clear of heavy understory.*

The brown-leggeds had their reasons. We would watch one meadow after a burn, and some time later, through the winter and into early summer when the elk were returning, the green of the grasses seemed so much brighter, as if two shoots had grown up for every one burned. Great herds of elk would loll around in the emerald sun. At the end of a summer of such grasses, the Indians had an easy hunt, a fat hunt. They would surround the elk and shoot.

The snow geese tell us that to the white two-leggeds, this policy of the brown two-leggeds with regard to fire would seem insane. The white two-leggeds don't know how to live with fire, say the snow geese. They prefer to suppress it. They think it's best not to let anything burn.

But then the tinder just builds and builds! We've seen it, we say.

Yes, the geese say. But the two-leggeds don't see it. They don't want to see it.

It will scald them, then, we say. It will reach out and sear them until they die.

Yes. But what are we to do?

Make them see it, we say. Make them see it.

Burning

BARBARA

I have a son. A son with sixty-five percent of his total body area burned. TBA: Total Body Area. Medical parlance. I have been infested with medical parlance.

His face suffered least, thank God. I think Thank God every time I see him, every time I see him again each morning. The right side will remain somewhat distorted, though, and he no longer has any hope of developing his dad's good looks. Black curly hair, yes—that will grow back—and the left eye faunlike, full of lash and black eyebrow. Both eyes retain their blue—a clear, almost royal color against the black lashes and black brows and white skin. But he will never be anybody's dream date, at least on the surface of things.

It's his hands I worry about most, though. I worry that they regain some semblance of function, that they don't pull and cripple back on themselves permanently, palsied fingers on otherwise functional arms. What a cruel fate for the child of two people obsessed with hand-work, his genes already gearing that way in his attention to fishing flies, his love of hammer and screwdriver, the small rugs he wove under my tutelage when he was six years old.

He wore no gloves when he fell in, no face covering either, come to think of it, both hands and face sliding in last. But somehow in the swirl of what must have felt like his own death, he kept his head above water, preserving it and bobbing up from the scald, *swimming* as if no matter what the temperature, our bodies still guard against drowning.

Yet to achieve this his hands had to pedal the cauldron. Steaming, shrieking, lobster claws going red and then gray. They told me they hoisted him up by coat, by forearm, grabbing denim and flannel, jerking him out until he lay in a cloud of steam and water on the asphalt. He did not move, did not open his eyes and smile, did not even breathe for a minute until a teacher put her mouth to his and blew. Other children cried, teachers ran for help, the ambulance began its scream up the mesa—while one elderly principal, who began his career at that school when my brother was in fifth grade, called me at home.

There is no voice like That Voice. It's the Voice you dread, waiting on winter evenings for your husband to make it home. The Voice you have nightmares about the first time you leave your children with someone else for the night. I knew it as soon as it said "Barbara," because I recognized Paul Carson, because I knew there was no sane reason he would call, because the tone was so deadly somehow, even though all he said was my name.

I slid the way Trent must have slid. Invertebrate, noodling toward some unfathomable bottom. The phone cord stretched long.

"Barbara? Barbara?"

But I had no capacity for words.

"I'll be right over," he said, and this elderly gentleman, working a year past retirement because they could not find a replacement, must have set his hat (an old tweed with a crease down the crown) on his head, and told his secretary to run tackle, because he was at my door in ten minutes.

He'd already said, There has been an accident. He'd already gone on about an open manhole and a game of kickball. He had begun talking about water, hot water, but that was the point at which I fell prey to all the sensory deprivation inherent in a woman buried deep in a cave, and could no longer hear or speak or function.

He arrived in a long tweed coat that matched his hat, wingtip shoes, tie neatly bound at the neck and peeping out through the collar of the coat. He looked for all the world like a distinguished college dean rather than an elementary principal in a small mountain town.

"Where's your coat?" he asked, glancing at my boots by the door.

I understood. His sureness, his firm command, found their way to my legs and joints, and I stumbled into my winter clothes.

"To the hospital?" I said, throat dry as the Sahara, windswept, without oasis.

He nodded. "Your husband will join you there."

His efficiency and thoughtfulness would have astonished me at any other time, did astonish me later when I sat up nights going over and over that day in my head. But at the time I merely bowed my head and followed him out to a well-maintained Buick, slate blue and as regal as himself.

Galveston. What did I think when I went there? Trent Sr. had volunteered to go with Trent, right away, while I stayed home with Brandon. We both knew I'd be down sometime soon, but that he, not I, would endure it better, and that he, not I, would, if he stayed home, bury himself in furniture-making to forget about his older son, and would likely neglect his younger in the process.

My first impression of the hospital at Galveston was whiteness. Whiteness, and then an antiseptic smell masking a deeper, more insidious odor, the odor of flesh burned and rotting off. Trent Sr. met me with eyes hollowed, cadaverous, eyes similar to those of the dead fish he brings home for dinner out of the La Plata River. "Thank God you are here," he whispered, clasping my hand and almost swaying into me. I held him. I held him, arms up around his neck, stroking the thick dark hair which lay there, damp. But over the mass of his shoulders, over the slumping slope of my husband's body, I saw the bed, hospital steel and white, the kind of bed that bends at the waist and did so then, cupping in its lounge the body of my son. He, too, stared at me, unblinking, though his eyes were those of a fish still alive, a fish alive and unable to move.

Trent Sr. rustled off me; I whispered some kindness to him, designed to remove him from the room while at the same time offering a rendezvous later on. He slipped from me, and alone, I approached my son. I put my hand ever so gently on the left side of his skull and started crying before I could help myself.

"Mom! Don't Mom! Don't cryyyyyy!!!"

I was so startled by his shrieking that I stopped cold, dropped my hand from his head, pulled back, my face white I'm sure, while this creature rocked back and forth and shrieked before me. "Trent... I..." but my words were tangled in a glue of mucus. Seconds later, right after it dawned on me to hit the nurse's button but before I got up the nerve to do it *(What kind of mother are you? Not even able to comfort your own son)*, a tall black woman swished through and landed at his bed.

"Tracy,..." Trent mouthed, and his relief at seeing her, and not me, almost made me cry again.

The next day, I sniveled in his room while she took him to the place where pieces of him sloughed off into a gentle whirlpool of warmish water. I could hear screams down the hall. My son? Or other people's sons and daughters, other people's children baked beyond recognition? I could only imagine how painful the sloughing procedure was, how painful everything was. At home, I'd tried to read on this, this subject of pediatric burns, but I could only endure a paragraph at a time, picked through here and there and read right before I did something distracting and purposeful, like go to the grocery store. Even then, I found myself stopped, mid-aisle, staring at boxes of macaroni and cheese, or rows of salad oil, seeing not those things before me—boxed and controlled food—but the twists of burn scars, distortions similar to those on a venerable juniper, yet hardly as magnificent.

Trent came back from his daily slough bath looking somehow a bit refreshed. Maybe it was the clean bandages, or the soothing feel of new ointment against his skin. Or maybe it was Tracy's long black fingers, nails a shiny red, perched on his shoulders. I winced at that.

I winced as she lifted him from the wheelchair, tucked him into bed. My chin dissolved, my face a face you might encounter in a hall of mirrors, or so it felt inside, everything dripping and slimy and falling apart.

"You sleep, baby," she said to Trent, in a sure Southern voice, "you sleep." To me she said, as she passed to the door, "Come out with me, Ms. MacIntosh." I puppied after her, trusting the only person around to be trusted, down the hall to the elevator, down to the cafeteria, and the relief of a cup of coffee.

"You see," she was saying, as I was still trying to orient, my head full of plane ride and elevator and giant hospitals and depleted husbands, "you got to know that every burn patient is a two-year-old. No matter how old they are. That's the first thing you got to know."

"What else do I have to know?" I wanted to sip my coffee but my hands would shake and she would see that. For the time being, I just smelled it, a smell strong enough to overcome the antiseptic rot so prevalent upstairs.

"You also have to know that every burn patient also becomes mighty dependent on their number one nurse. I get sick? Man, you should see the raft of sh— junk I get when I come back. Hysterical parents. Even more hysterical children. So don't feel too bad if Trent right now is on to me more than anybody. That's normal."

I couldn't hold back tears anymore. My hall-of-mirrors face shattered completely and I started sobbing into the steam from the coffee. "But I'm his *mother!*"

His mother!

She put a slender hand on my wrist. "I know you are, sweetheart. And I know you're a good one at that."

"You do?"

"You bet. I see a lot of kids in here, Ms. MacIntosh. And a lot of parents. I can tell which kids got good parents, and which don't."

I looked up, sniffing into this small redemption. "I just wish, I just wish I could do something." My words sounded so trite, so common, that I wished I hadn't said them. But Tracy was nodding.

"In a couple of days, you can. Once you get used to it here. Maybe you can go with us to the whirlpool. I think Trent'd like that."

"Tracy, Ms...." I squinted at her name tag. "Miss Johnson, I can't even read three sentences on burns without losing my nerve. I make it through every day just glad my husband didn't fight coming down here, so that I could stay home most of the time and watch my other son, and do my work, and know that my husband isn't feeding his arm to a band saw because he's so distraught over Trent. *I don't know what I can do here.*" I felt like adding, *What good am I?* but she just smiled.

"My mama felt the same way when I was young."

"What? What do you mean?"

She never let her eyes lose mine, but she took her right hand and rolled up her left sleeve. The swirl of a burn scar began to emerge. "It's sizable," she said. "It goes onto my back." And while I stared at it, she said, "You see, Ms. MacIntosh, I been right where your son is. And a part of me has never left."

I had to wear hospital scrubs and a mask and gloves to go with Trent to the sloughing. A large, stainless steel tub in the shape of an oval sat in the middle of a white-tiled room. I had to stand back some distance, while Tracy unwrapped him and I witnessed the gutted fish of my son, the ghastly resemblance to my uncle's butchered cows, strung up and skinned in preparation for curing. I'd seen bits and pieces of Trent prior to this, an arm here, a leg there, but this was the first time I had seen the entire thing, and I had to duck my head to prevent myself from vomiting. Then I had to leave the room, because it was unbearable that this was my son, my oldest boy, the one I had birthed and done everything in my power to protect. My protection, I could see in the live tissue glistening with exposed fat, the raw meat look of the butcher shop, was useless. The Great Mother could do nothing against some idiot who left a manhole cover off at lunchtime. All this time I'd been afraid of him drowning in the river, or being leapt upon by a cougar while hiking, or falling prey to some pervert as he walked home from school. All this time I'd been looking in the wrong place. I sent him somewhere every day that was supposed to be safe. And I couldn't do a damn thing when it wasn't.

I heard him slide in the bath, and I slunk back in. He and Tracy were talking.

"I never talked to a black person before you," he said, wincing as Tracy moved him. His eyes had the lidded look I knew now was the effect of morphine.

"No? Not a black person, ever?" She gently swished the water with her hand. "What, they don't have 'em up there in Colorado?"

"Um, well, Denver, I guess." He winced again, words cutting through gasps of breath, clenched teeth. I could tell he talked as a way to keep back pain. Later, he'd tell me about the snow geese, how they came and feathered him, soothed their whiteness over his dead gray cells and his live red ones. Later, he'd say, you're right, Mom, I talked to help it, and that helped along with the shots Tracy gave me. But then there were the geese.

The geese? I'd ask. And he'd tell me. He'd tell me the most private thing I knew I would ever know about him.

Tracy kept swishing. "But there's not any black folks in La Plata," she said.

"Naw. La Plata's full of Spics and Indians and old white farts, but not black people."

"Well, I never talked to an Indian. Except, my great-grandmother's supposed to be Choctaw."

"So you *are* Indian... Ow!"

"Sorry, but I gotta do this."

Tears clouded my eyes so much I had to leave again. My son! A cooked fish. A boy more aware of race and country than I ever would have guessed.

I let them dry off together, knowing I could not stand to look at the whole body of him, out of the tub, again. I heard them laugh. I heard him say, "They got lots of black people in Galveston?" And her saying, "Uh-huh. It's in the South."

"The South? What's that mean?"

"The South is where they had slaves. Black people were slaves."

There was a bit of silence. Surely Trent knew that? Then he said, "Oh, yeah."

I stood right outside the door. In minutes it swished open, and they emerged. I smiled down at him; he smiled at me.

"Was that okay, Mom?" he asked.

"It was okay, sweetie," I said. I realized he had no idea I'd been out of the room most of the time.

"Tracy says the South is where they had slaves."

Tracy's eyes and mine wavered at each other. A ball of wax formed in my throat. "That's right, Trent."

"That was a terrible thing, right?"

"Right, Trent."

Tracy's hand rested on his shoulder, just as it did the first day I saw her with him. We stood still in the hallway, that uncanny ability of children to spot the unspoken shame of adults quivering all around us.

How did he do that, sick as he was? How did he have the wherewithal, through morphine and excruciating pain and the horrendous appearance of his body, to register in on slavery? I shook my head.

Tracy seemed to have the same thought. "Damn, child," she said softly, kicking the wheelchair into gear. "You gonna make it just fine."

SARAH

In the basement he tells me everything is going to be just fine. In this kind of voice that reminds me of a cat's purr. I don't have any clothes on.

He's got photographic equipment. He takes all kinds of pictures. Pictures of me alone, pictures of him with me. Those last ones are on a timer, I know that; it's the same thing he uses when he takes pictures of the family on picnics. Mom loves those pictures; she's always going on about how good he is with a camera.

Click click flash. A dozen flashes. Each one a different pose. I would be cold but *I've left again. I... She arches her back, thrusting her chest into the air. Next he tells her to open her legs, and then zooms in to that spot between them, that spot he loves to touch. He would stimulate her there until she was red and swollen. It made her sore but sometimes it felt good. She hates herself the most when it feels good. She can't understand how it can feel good when everything else about it feels so bad. She must be as sick as he is.*

"This is for the family," he says, focusing. "See, people want to see pictures of you. They'll pay us for it."

"F...for the family?" *I hear her say. She's weak, barely alive. A shell person like he is. But she—she has to pretend that she's there. That she's okay.*

"Sarah, do you know how much this house cost?"

She shakes her head. I shake my head, but Dad is always going on about how, when he was growing up, *his mother would give him a quarter to buy bread and a gallon of milk and would tell him to bring back the change. He's upset that things aren't that cheap anymore. That things aren't the way they were in the Depression.*

"This house cost thirty thousand dollars. Can you believe it?" He sounds disgusted, as if the world were out to get him. *He readjusts his lens.* "So this will help pay for things for the family."

She's a ghost now, not even there. Up on the ceiling, where he can't get to her. He can't know that but he must see something hollow in her because he says, "It's important to think of others, Sarah."

The think-of-others stuff comes from her—my—grandmother, from his own mother. And from generations of teachers and preachers her grandmother says were doing God's work in the world. Didn't she know her great-aunt Edna died in New Guinea, a missionary? Or that Martin Luther Graves was a Presbyterian minister who taught college? My grandmother had been a teacher too, before she got married, and now she goes to church all the time and weeps. I can never figure out the tears because the rest of the time my grandmother wears a hard line on her mouth and calls us all *selfish for not joining her in God and then in heaven when she finally dies.*

My grandmother lives in California and we see her about once a year. *Dad tries to please her no end. He won't even drink a beer in her presence.* When I asked Mom about that Mom whispered that Grandma's father was an alcoholic and so she hated anyone to drink in front of her.

Selfish people drank, and hurt others.

"So you see, Sarah? These will help out. People want to see you. They'll pay. And it'll be just fine."

She goes back to posing. He comes and she kneels in front of him and sticks his penis in her mouth. Click flash. He's hard and she sucks.

~~*Feels good, oh it feels good doesn't it Sarah?*~~

Yes Daddy yes Daddy stomach curdling head on the ceiling crotch aroused even though she's gagging.

But she loves her daddy, and if you love someone you never, ever hurt them.

Ricky draws dirty pictures with magic markers underneath the coffee table the next afternoon. "Sarah's pussy," he labels one drawing. In another, he draws huge tits. Then a man's penis, then a pair of buttocks. All dismembered, all parts of bodies. I ignore all these things because I can't stand what they say. Because it means Ricky knows, *my brother knows and stomach curdle gag all over again.*

The only non-sex things he tries to draw are earmuffs. He can draw one side, but when he carries the line over to the other side of the muff, it ends up coiling and spiraling, so the two don't match. I show him a picture of Picasso so that he won't be so mad they didn't turn out right. "See? He's got both eyes on one side of that lady's head." I'm always trying to calm him down.

It doesn't matter. The muffs don't turn out the way he wants them to.

"Oh, that's gooood, Sarah," he says in a high-pitched, whiny, nasty tone. "Fuck you."

He throws the markers all over the carpet and runs from the room.

The next Sunday the Denver *Post* runs a story about a family whose house has been firebombed. I read every word of it. I'm hooked on it, especially on two facts: that the firebomb was thrown by somebody mad at the dad (of course), and that two kids, an older brother and a younger, were the only ones who escaped. They did that by climbing out on the roof with wet blankets over them and sliding down the gutter to the ground. But four other kids died, along with the parents.

I go over and over the escape route in my mind. I think about the older boy running into the younger one's room, soaking blankets, grabbing him and pushing him out the window onto the slanty roof. I think about how carefully they must have had to make their way across that steep part and over to where the house joined the garage and the gutter ran down. I think about how I would escape, lying on my bed with the red print curtains Mom made billowing over me from the open window. I go outside and look at the distance between the window and the ground.

About five or six feet. Could I make it if I had to jump? Probably. But I don't want to hurt myself, break any bones.

I read in a side article to the bomb story about what to do to protect yourself from fire. One thing they suggest includes sleeping with the door closed. I shake my head. I can't do that. I can't see that way. It doesn't matter anyway—the door—won't stop—*But at least, with it open, she can see him coming. At least it's one less heart attack she has to cope with, since total surprise is gone.* Still, I hate the idea of a fire, real fire. So I make a deal with the suggestion in the article and leave the door partway shut. Not all the way open, but not shut either. Light streams in on seams that way. Moonbeams show up lumps of clothing and turn them into monsters. And sometimes the heart attack comes anyway, the feeling of Dad's eyes beading in, the knob turning—and with this goes me, shattering into a million bits, like windowpanes do when the fire inside gets too hot and they explode out into the air.

Picnic

SARAH

Mrs. MacIntosh asks me to go on a picnic with them once it starts to warm up in the afternoons. Trent's decided to like me, I guess. We have a good time in his room on those Wednesdays waiting for Ricky to get done with his piano lessons, and sometimes when we laugh I see Mrs. MacIntosh peeking in the room as if she can't believe what she's hearing. She's a cool lady, Mrs. MacIntosh, only sometimes she makes me nervous because her eyes get all hollow and needy like Mom's. But I think it's because of what happened to Trent. At least I hope so.

Anyway, she asks me on a picnic. I ask Mom and she says, Yes, when we drive into Safeway on Saturday to go to the store, I'll drop you off. So that Saturday I get up and go take a shower. I keep the bathroom door locked because I don't want anybody in here. Mom'll come in sometimes. She always takes a bath with the door open. Sometimes she asks me if I want her bath water when she's done, but I think that's gross.

When I get done with the shower, I look for my comb but when I don't find it I think that I must have left it in my room. So I have to go out and get it. I wrap my towel—the biggest one I can find—really carefully around me. I tuck in the end under my armpit so it can't fall off. *Nobody can see.* It's bad enough, walking down the hall in a towel.

I get to my bedroom, grab the comb, go back. But when I get there, she's there. She's there in her flimsy gown even though it's still cold in the mornings and she says sex is for only after you're married. She flaunts things every chance she gets. I can see her—her pussy,

Ricky's word—all I can think of even though it leaves a taste like metal in my mouth that I want to spit out. *Pussy pussy pussy*, so angry, all of his anger at *it, her, it,* Mine?

She sits down on the toilet.

"Mom," I say, "I wasn't done in here."

"Well, I need to take a shower."

She can say things just so. Well, *I* need to take a shower. Like that. If I push it more she'll just say I've been in here long enough and it's her house anyway.

Pee goes into the toilet. She wipes herself, stands up, flushes. If I let my eyes go where they naturally go, I look right at her—at her—

Tits. Anger word. Ricky's word. *Boobs.* Ridicule word. *Bosoms.* Mom's word. She giggles it sideways out of her mouth, like when we're at restaurants. "Heavens," she'll say, "look at the bosoms on *that* woman." I blush to magenta when she says stuff like that and I don't even want to look at Ricky.

Bosoms. Her bosoms. They crowd at me.

She turns on the water for the shower. "You can keep doing what you're doing, honey," she says, getting in.

I can't comb my hair in a foggy mirror. But it's no use. *And I'll never let you see ME naked. Never.* She would hate me. She would see and then hate me about…about…the basement…the fire…

She might kill me. Even if I never wanted it…the fire…the lab coat fingers… Never, never wanted it.

My body.

She hates.

My body.

On the picnic I peek at Mrs. MacIntosh. We're up by Turtle Lake and the sun makes a halo of light around her frizzy blonde hair, like the angel Dad puts on the tree every year. Mom and Dad named that angel Lo because when I was little I asked Mom who Lo was, and Mom said, What do you mean, and I said, you know, Lo the angel of the Lord. Mom started laughing.

But Mrs. MacIntosh is much better than Lo. She smiles and talks to Brandon, who sits next to her oozing some kind of jealousy. Trent is between me and his dad. Brandon glares at Trent, who's too busy eating chicken to notice. But I recognize that glare; it's the glare of the baby brother who finally gets some kind of attention he thinks only the oldest one gets. I roll my eyes. Ricky does the same thing. He thinks Mom and Dad like me only. I can't believe he's that stupid, because the kind of attention I get is not exactly like winning the Miss America pageant. But it's also true that he's left-handed and good at stuff they're not, like picking up Spanish and songs by ear. Anything they haven't learned from all their degrees they don't know what to do with.

I stick my tongue out at Brandon and help myself to another piece of chicken. Brandon sticks his tongue out back, fast, while his mom turns to ask for the potato salad. Our blanket's an old packing quilt smack in the middle of the meadow south of the lake. On either side rise red sandstone cliffs full of oak and ponderosa, and I can still see big patches of snow on them.

Brandon looks like Trent might have before he got burned. It's not that Trent's face is entirely messed up, but the right side has some bad scars that push his face around and make it hard for me to think what his normal face ever looked like, although I saw a picture of him from last year up on the mantelpiece. His hair has grown back, and it's a dark mop like his dad's, curly and thick with just a little bit of his mom's blonde hair that shows up in the bright sun. Brandon's hair is darker, too, like his dad, though not as dark as Trent, and he has his mom's freckles and smaller nose and chin. I guess that Trent has some of that look too, because his left eye is beautiful, like a fawn's, and his left jawline fine and sharp.

Of course, that could all shift when he grows up: you don't ever see a kid with Mr. MacIntosh's saggy cheeks, or his kind of strong nose. Still, Mr. MacIntosh isn't ugly. He's kind of handsome. I love the amount of hair growing on his arms. It makes little swirls here and there, and his hands are wide and tough from making furniture all the time. When I've eaten dinner at their house before, I've seen him wink across the table at Mrs. MacIntosh, and he does it again, now.

I have to stop chewing my drumstick, it makes me feel so good, that wink. I try to hold that feeling there forever. While I'm doing this the sun beams on my head and the grasses don't even breathe and I don't even think anybody else talks, either, though I wouldn't know. I'm a million miles into that feeling.

BARBARA

Sarah gives me a good feeling. Shoulder-length brown hair, bluish eyes with yellow flecks in them that make me think they're almost turquoise, a tall skinny girl beginning to get that coltish appearance so common in the couple of years before adolescence. She dives into the fried chicken I made and I realize that until she came along, I had been Trent's one true friend, as well as his mother and Brandon's mother and Trent Sr.'s wife and a weaver.

It's not that I don't enjoy his friendship. Trent and I play cards in the early afternoons before Brandon comes home from school. We sit on his bed and dish out kings and queens and aces. He teaches me poker, a game his father must have revealed to him, though he claims all the boys at school circle round and lay bets when the teachers aren't looking. I teach him rummy and hearts, and we laugh quietly, there on his sleigh bed with the Denver Broncos posters looming over it.

But I'll never be someone his age, never substitute for that kind of friendship, nor do I want to. But Sarah! After eating the picnic, I take the three of them to the edge of the lake where the willow grows and cut a stalk. "Split-twig figurines," I say, and my boys say, "You mean like those horses you make?" And I nod. I used to put one in their stockings every Christmas.

"We should have greener willow, spring willow, but this will do," I say.

"We could wait a month," Brandon says.

"No," Trent says. "I want to do this now."

Sarah looks puzzled. "What's a split-twig figurine?"

"Something the Indians used to make. I'll show you."

So I cut a stalk, lop off the floppy top to the point where I have a small platform of willow I can notch. I sit down on a grassy patch on the shore and cut into it, then split the stalk lengthwise, all the way down, holding one side in my teeth, the other between my two thumbs, the tension perfect or otherwise the split will tear off short. I stop with about three inches to go from the base.

My children and Sarah stand around me, watching. "Now," I say, "this is what you do." And I take both halves of the twig and bend them until they form the beginnings of an outline of an animal, with a back leg (where the unsplit base is, and where I start), and a backbone. At the shoulder, I take one half of the stalk down for a front leg, bending it back at the base and keeping it going back up to start the neck. I hold it to the shoulder while I take the other strand and wrap it, front leg to hind leg, mummy style, five or six times till it forms a body. Then I tuck the end of that strand up inside the wrapping, toward the neck I've started with the other strand. I take that other strand, form the neck exactly the way I formed the front leg, bending at the top this time and sending the twig back down to form a loop over the body behind the shoulder. Then back up again, into a triangular head, wrapping around the head, then back down, mummy style again, along the neck. I tuck the end up under the neck wrappings.

"Voilá," I say. "Split-twig figurine."

"A split *fig twig*urine." Trent laughs.

"I wanna do that!" Brandon grabs the willow animal and inspects it.

"Okay, okay." So I cut them all stalks of their own, wading back into the thicket with its aging red winter color and the buds barely formed. Brandon is right; in a month the stalks will have a fur of green.

We practice splitting them. Then I watch as they fumble around the strips, small hands trying to manipulate long strands. Trent, his splints off, hands still retracted but not as badly as before, struggles to make his fingers form the body, fights to hold onto one strip while wrapping with the other. The doctors tell me all the time to get him doing things like this, to stretch and bend the skin around his hands, but sometimes he grows so frustrated that he begins to cry and I call it quits. He doesn't let me help him; if I try to help he seems to feel that he's failed.

He bends over farther and farther into the willow in his hands. I can't see his face and I know he doesn't want me to. The willow keeps springing out, a wiry hair gone AWOL.

"Here," Sarah says, out of the blue. I've forgotten about her because I have been so focused on Trent, and she has been so quiet. "I'll hold that while you wrap it."

And he lets her. He lets her reach over and pinch her thumb and forefinger at the point where the front leg strand meets the shoulder, and he wraps up the body. He's able to form the neck and head then, stumbling only over the tight wraps over the head. Again, Sarah helps him, but only until he gets down to the neck again.

"Ta-da!" Sarah says, when he finishes. "Hold it up, Trent."

Trent holds it up. I smile and Trent smiles. Then I sniff, and he sniffs.

Sarah's face takes on the color of sea water. "What's wrong? Did I do something wrong?"

I reach for her and hug her. "No, honey, you did everything just right." There is no way I can explain the tears behind our smiles, different tears for different reasons, but tears nonetheless.

Sarah and Trent and Brandon bolt away after that, dissipating into the atmosphere the way children always do. I can hear their shouts and calls back behind the willow in the matted meadow where our picnic blanket lies. Trent Sr. stands up the lake a bit, fishing as ever. A flutter of wings whiffles off behind me, where Sarah and Trent had been sitting. I turn.

Two snow geese ascend into the air, batting their wings toward spring.

Music

Finally, a nice week of spring weather. By the third day, I have all the windows open and I'm cleaning. When I got married I made a vow to clean in the first warm days after the long winter. Usually that's in March sometime, when the weather teases us with some good afternoons, and then goes back to being winter for another month or so. By noon today, it's too lovely to stay cooped up inside, so I wash all my quilts and now I'm airing out the place. I put the quilts out on the line for a few hours and then go out and beat them come late afternoon, right before the sun starts falling and the temperature goes with it. Days like this, there's forty degrees between three p.m. and three a.m.

The Graves kids play next door, back from school. I keep the corner of one eye on them through all the quilt dust. It's about four o'clock, another hour or so till dusk, till their dad comes home and they disappear for dinner. Sometimes I hear faint piano music coming from the basement, and I suppose one or both of them have lessons. Walt took lessons when he was a kid, as he always did have an ear for music. But Ted, never, and I guess I felt that music was a blessing and a gift, but not something mandatory for living out here. If you had to make parlor music back east, well then I would think about it. Some of the mothers of my childhood friends pretended to that kind of fashion, but nothing seemed more ridiculous to me than a bunch of ladies drinking tea out of rose-laden china cups, all dressed up with nowhere to go but across the long dusty drives of one another's homesteads. By the time they came to the door, the hems of their skirts were cluttered with dust, their shoes no longer shiny and black.

My mother, though, did play. She played beautifully, but she also rode a horse meaner than most cowboys could and cooked meals for a hundred on occasion. Out of her, piano-playing seemed less like an affectation designed to acquire society and more like—well, as with everything else she did—one of her queer passions. In Colorado with the boys, though, where we first lived in the tent at Philistine Mine, and then out here before there was much in the way of other houses, I always thought it was more important they learn how to hunt, how to ski, how to read animal sign and know which way was north. Of course, I told them education was important, because I believe in democracy, and I believe in furthering the mind. I used to fill them with stories of Thomas Jefferson and James Madison and Alexander Hamilton on cold winter nights when they tired of the Bible.

I squint into the sun disappearing over the ridge as I finish beating my quilt. When Walt was old enough, he questioned me on democracy, asked why even aim for it when it was bound to fail at some level. This was during the Depression, and he was already at work for the CCC. If I recall, I pursed my lips, sat my hands together on my apron, and said, We-ell, it's like a worthy marriage. You may never get it perfect, but the point is to die trying.

Clothespins in my mouth, I try to remember if Walt said anything at all to that. Later on, he would tell me that was one of the wisest things he ever heard me say, and one of the toughest. But that was when his marriage was ending and he was struggling so hard to figure out whether it was "worthy" or not. He thought I'd kill him for wanting a divorce.

I smile, the way you always smile about your kids when you're remembering something fine and sensible and sweet about them. But one of the Graves kids yelps then and breaks my thoughts. I look over. Mrs. Graves comes out. I don't see her much. She stays in the house a lot, or drives off into town herky-jerky style, as if she never did quite figure out how to use a clutch. She's a tall woman, angular, with short brown hair and glasses. She moves like an ostrich I saw once at the state fair, and I hope for Sarah's sake that the girl learns how to be more at home in her body.

Mrs. Graves has got a gardener's claw in her hand, and she moves toward a strip of dirt lining the patio. Grooming for flowers, I guess. Sarah and Ricky are playing whiffle ball. Ricky pitches and Sarah connects, whacking it down the slope toward the road.

"Oooh," she says, "I got you good!"

Mrs. Graves lifts her head from the bed of dirt she has been combing. "Sarah, use correct English, please."

That's all she says. Then she lowers her head in fine ostrich fashion, buckling back in toward her patch of dirt. She doesn't see her daughter's shoulders square off, the willful setting of her carriage against her mother's words. She doesn't see them playing ball. She didn't even greet them when she came outside. She is wholly absorbed in churning up the dirt.

What else doesn't she see? And why do I get the unsettling feeling—standing here with a quilt half folded and clothespins dropping into the bucket—that despite appearances, she is nowhere near being present on planet Earth?

I fold my quilts and go back inside. Later, come dusk, I return to the yard for my bucket of clothespins. I've got my red agate arrowhead, smooth in my hand.

The Graves' basement window remains open even though it's getting chilly out. Piano music seeps from it. The music tinges the air, lacy fingers through the trees. I pause, listen, my hand still on the agate point. Beethoven's *Für Elise*. It's that precious hour, past sunset, when the world is vacant and still and full. The cottonwoods stand naked, stick-like, as they have all winter. Sound carries far and tinnily in air like this.

"Saarrah! Dinner!"

The music stops. A faraway clop of steps. My heart joins in with the silence left by her music, the way it used to when I knew they were going to blast a bit more out of the Philistine Mine. Why am I waiting for bombs to go off? I shake my head, and close my door against the blackening night.

Piano music. Similar to what used to come out of the Kittredge Saloon on a Saturday night when we Utes camped diagonally across from it. We used to do that when the government rations came in. Then we'd leave as soon as possible. We didn't like that town.

The piano music here is slower, though, not something you'd play for a pack of drunk white miners in town to blow their week's pay. This is the kind of music I heard when President Grant took me to what he called "the symphony." That's the first and last time I ever heard a "symphony."

Something moves in the dark below me, on the side lawn. I'm feeling kind of soothed again, and I'm about to think the thing that moved is just a deer and close my eyes for the night, but there's something funny about it. It's fatter than a deer. And whiter. It's almost dark so I can't really see much. I stare at it awhile, till the outline becomes clear. It's a woman, a fat woman, with her arms crossed. There is something very familiar about her but I can't make out her features and she doesn't move. She just stands there, gazing at the Graves' house like she's trying to figure it out. Like horses sometimes gaze at the grass, or the sun going down.

The smallest scent of lilacs seeps up into my crevice. Never had lilacs till the whites came, but I liked them. But lilacs now? It's too early for them. Not till May, at least. I sniff again. Fake lilacs. White lady lilacs. All the white women wore that scent back then, still did when I haunted Lars.

The figure moves, turning her back on the Graves' place. I start. My skull actually bangs on the crevice wall. Oodegaard? Is that Mrs. Oodegaard? All of a sudden I see the arrowhead, clear as day, and I can feel her hands caressing it, pillowy old white lady fingers.

Mrs. Oodegaard! I want to call. And a second later, I want to call,

Where's Lars? But she's out of my line of sight, a fat old elk moving off into the shadows. I hear a door close, and for some reason I don't think Lars waits on the other side of it.

Lars has been on my mind far too long, I realize that night after the wind rolls my bones again for a good long time. Got a guilty conscience about him, about that whole haunting business. It didn't end up fairly. Didn't end up well. Lars was some kind of creature I'd never seen. After the time he went on about zoos and such and laughed at me, I stayed away a good while. In all my time of being a warrior and a negotiator, not even Congress and their stupid questions humiliated me quite as much as Lars. Congress at least had power. Had a huge amount of it. But here was Lars, a skinny bookkeeper for a rotten silver mine, with not a stick of power to his name. Not that kind, anyway.

In late summer, when the purple asters and little yellow daisies were blooming, I dared to look for him again. I didn't look very hard at first, but Philistine was a small place and there weren't too many places to look. I stumbled on him at dusk, slumped over his desk as if he were sleeping. I was afraid to find him in the same mood as last time, but that day Lars seemed different, and even though I still didn't expect to make much of an impact, I decided to give it a try. Life was getting dull otherwise.

I slipped inside the shack and brushed Lars' shoulder like a light breeze.

"Wake up," I said.

"Un-huh," said Lars, and dropped his head back down on the desk.

I spotted a Bible underneath Lars' hand. Lars' finger had closed around Genesis, as if before he collapsed he'd thought he might read the Bible again, start to finish. White folks did that a lot back then— sought out the Bible as if it would tell them the answer to anything. I had a sudden flash that perhaps, just perhaps, Lars was looking for spiritual help. I hesitated for mere seconds while admonishments from my tribal upbringing attempted to float toward consciousness. But the brilliance of the opportunity won out, and the admonishments receded like drowning hands protesting from under water.

"Evolution is correct," I whispered. I couldn't help but smirk. This was ingenious. In my spare time, loitering outside waiting to haunt, I read newspapers discarded in the tall mesh trash basket just outside Lars' office. I never liked to read much, because if you read then you stop listening, and it's better to listen. Lose your memory otherwise. White people have the lousiest memories.

But after my trip to Washington I made an effort to read better. Too much going on, too many scientists and people coming to my tribe to "study" us and then telling us we were stupid.

So in the newspapers outside Lars' office I found out about "evolution," about a Scopes Monkey Trial. I didn't understand the trial—the American legal system never made much sense to me—but evolution was another thing. I couldn't believe this was something to get upset about. From what I could see, Charles Darwin was the first white man ever to really pay attention to what our animal and plant brothers and sisters might have to tell us, even if he did it in a funny sort of way. He even dared to suggest humans were subject to the same forces of nature as everyone else. Why so many Christians saw this as a threat to the very existence of a Great Spirit mystified me; after all, the Utes had a similar creation story, though it was far more sophisticated, what with Sinewav the Creator trying to make a land where people would not fight each other. But why change through time (which is all evolution seemed to be, when you got right down to it) should in any way contradict this was beyond me.

I shook my head. Lars had not responded to my first statement. "Evolution is correct," I whispered again, more loudly.

This time Lars sat up. "Hello? Who's there?"

"Do you forget about me in between times?"

Lars put his hands over his eyes and sighed. "No. Of course not."

Lars' eyes were red-rimmed, bloodshot, and exhausted. He'd run his fingers through his hair so many times that strands of it flew off at odd angles. His lips were parched and he kept licking them.

"I have a degree from a Bible college," said Lars. "You're just an Indian. What do you know about evolution?"

It was my turn to sigh. I was getting sick of this white man superiority shit. But I held off for the time being. "What do you think about it, about evolution?" I asked.

"I think it's bunk."

I was quiet a minute. Then I said, "Stay where you are. I'll be right back."

Lars shrugged and fell to his desk again. Outside, I walked to the nearest fir and picked up a cone from the ground underneath it. I came back and held it up to Lars' face.

"What's this?" I asked.

"A pine cone."

"What kind?"

"I don't kn—" Lars looked harder. "A Doug fir."

"Very good. Now, see these little tails that stick out between the scallops of the cone?"

"Ye-s." Lars touched one of them. They were slightly curled and forked at the bottom.

"We Utes have a story about them."

Lars blinked and propped his forehead against a long hand. "Go on," he said.

"Okay. You know how mice eat the seeds of the cone? The seeds are tucked up under these scallops now, but in old days the scallops didn't used to be flat and were more open, like on a ponderosa cone. Do you know what I mean?"

Lars nodded, taking the fir cone in his free hand. "They had space underneath them. These don't."

"Right. Well, every year the mice would eat all the seeds. They ate so many that the trees didn't have enough to reproduce. So they begged the mice. They said, Next year, leave us a few seeds. Just a few in every cone. Okay, said the mice. They meant well. But mice are mice. They don't think when they're eating. They just eat. So the next year they forgot all about their promise and ate all the seeds again."

I paused and glanced at Lars. He still had droopy eyes, but he was listening. I resumed. "We're going to start dying off, said the trees to the mice, If you don't cut it out.

"Oh yes, yes, said the mice. We're sorry. We'll be better next year.

"But they weren't better next year. The trees watched as the mice munched and munched and stored and stored the seeds for winter. The trees began to panic. Their panic took the form of a great wind, the kind that is vast and makes you, if you happen to be under it at the time, feel very small and helpless. They talked through the wind, needles whistling and moaning. But after a few minutes their panic subsided and they were able to think of a solution."

"What'd they do?" asked Lars.

"Ah," I said. I took the cone out of Lars' hand. "Let this be a warning to you, mice, said the trees. And before the mice could move..." my fist clenched around the cone, "...they snapped their scallops shut over the mice, so that nothing but their tails showed."

Lars stared at the cone. I tickled a little tail. "And that's why the Douglas fir cones are flat and have tails."

Silence. Then Lars asked, "So the mice don't get any food anymore?" He seemed profoundly dismayed.

I laughed. "Of course they do. But the cones limit it. They snap shut every year at a certain time, and the mice see the tails and know better now."

"I see," said Lars.

I tossed the cone on Lars' desk. "Think about it. *That,* my friend, is a story about evolution."

"Jeez, ya stupid Injun. You don't go fuckin' with a guy's head like that."

A sharp stick jabbed me in the belly. I'd been dozing on the scree slope in the afternoon sun. "Huh-nuh?" I blinked awake. Silhouetted against the sky was a man with a fiddle, one leg, and a beard.

"Who are you?" I asked, scrambling to an upright position as fast as I could.

The fiddler smirked. "Ya know, you're not the only damn ghost around here. Tom Heaney's me name. Died twenty years ago, summer of '05, in this damn mine. Been here a lot longer than you have."

"Then how come I haven't seen you?"

"'Cause, ya stupid Injun, I live in the *mine*. Ya know, the place you won't go? I died in there. But it scares the bejeesus out of you, saw that the first day you come here. Shit." He spat a stream of tobacco juice onto the rocks.

I stood taller. I didn't have time for people who called me a stupid Injun. "You want me to talk to you, stop calling me bad names. My name is Chief Ouray."

"Yeah," said Tom, not batting an eye, "and I'm the queen's underpants."

"I *am*." I splayed my legs and crossed my arms in what I knew was a stereotypical Indian-brave pose. But if it, along with a stony face, made the fiddler back down, then I would use it.

"Okay, okay," said Tom. "You're Chief Ouray. But I hafta tell you something."

"What?"

"Leave Oodegaard alone."

"What? Why?"

"'Cause he's disturbed enough as it is. 'Cause he's the wrong man to haunt. But most of all 'cause he nearly killed himself last night after you got done with him."

"What?"

"Yup. Walked right into that shaft wonkin' about evolution. Jesus, Mary and Joseph! Evolution! Now where'd he get a cockamamie idea like that, eh? Reading too many papers, I thought, till he started goin' on about mice and pine cones and what 'The Indian' said, and then I knew it was you."

"How'd you know about me?"

Tom sighed. "Thick skull ya got, eh? And they said you were intelligent." He spat. "Like I said, you ain't the only ghost around here. You're just the only one who won't go in the mines. All the other ghosts—mostly tommyknockers, but there's me, and Bart, the haunted tram car—live in the mines. So ya don't know about us. But we know about you. You bet."

"Tommyknockers?"

Tom rolled his eyes. "You know. Friendly spirits. Keep the miners going. Not scary ones, like me."

"Oh," I said. It was unsettling to discover that not only was I out of it in the living world—land taken and battered and molded into something foreign—but that the dead walking around were of a different order too. I thought up until then that the only dead folk were my own people. Tommyknockers? Fiddle players? Where were my people?

But I knew. Every time my spirit left Philistine and flew back to my hill-gazing skull, I heard them. They were a collective moaning across the valley; they were the apocryphal voice in the wind. Their grief throbbed as an undercurrent in everything—river sucks and stream whirls; the sudden crack of a rock sliding down hill; low thunder. Oh yes, I knew where they were and what they looked like: mouth-O's, sunken cheeks, skin covered in measles or the boils of smallpox, hair butchered in mourning, flesh-offerings leaving wounds in their forearms. There were women in funeral shrouds, and children blowing away, cell by cell, in the disintegrating winds that tunneled into their burial cracks. And men, men like myself, were beaten and tattered, their sole remaining echo that of their spearpoints, which littered the ground for cowboy children to find after a good rain. I needed only to touch on their excruciating presence (and in fact a touch was all I could stand), and I'd be in Philistine, seeking refuge in the distraction of its activity, and revenge in the vulnerability of Lars.

"Well?" Tom glared at me.

"Well what?"

"You nearly sent Lars Oodegaard to his death. He's a preacher, ya know. Spent four years in college on the high end of a childhood that believed the same—that God did it in seven days. Now, he couldn't find steady work as a preacher. But till this mania took hold a him, he felt pretty safe in the world. But he don't feel safe now."

The fiddler, half a head shorter than me, came up and bunched a fist around my buckskin collar. "Ya don't fuck with a man's foundation like that. 'Specially when it's not so strong to begin with."

I started to push him away but Tom let go, violently.

"Now, I'm goin' to tell ya what happened. He came in that mine delirious. It's like he had no energy and wild energy all at once. His limbs moved like they were dead, eh? But his eyes shone in the dead black and his lips moved, mumbling on and on, weighin' his education versus your notion of the truth, finally screaming he didn't know which way was up. And that's when I knew he come in there to die. He just wanted to step right off into a shaft." He paused, wiping his brow on his shirt sleeve. "So I rescued him."

I caught myself listening whether I wanted to or not. "What'd you do?" I asked.

Fiddler held up his instrument to the sun. "Played," he said.

"What?"

"Hell, man, I can't physically pull the man away. I've got only one leg. I bled to death under a rotten timber. But music can shift your mood in a second, eh? So I played. I played the most cheerful-sounding Irish jig me ma ever taught me. I played it fast and sassy, and what do you know but he jerked his head up, horrified-like, and ran from that mine, all the way back to his wife. And she held his head while he cried, and cried, and cried, like a newborn baby."

Fire

SARAH

I'm supposed to be at the library while Mom gets her hair cut but I heard music again the other day out of the Kittredge and I want to go down there. The hotel is my favorite building next to the round-house in the rail yard. A plaque outside of it says it was built in the 1880s, and that "outlaws and dignitaries alike" stayed there when the Wild West was in full swing. In the lobby is a picture of it taken not too long after it opened, and the brown old tones of the photo don't take away from it at all. It's five stories of red brick, with white curly-cue trim. In the picture there's also three Ute teepees, camped catty-corner across from it, and they don't take away from it either. I'd have loved to live back then, with so many different types of people running around.

Soon as Mom drops me off at the library, I push my books through the Return slot and walk down to Main Street. It's early in the afternoon, kind of breezy and quiet. I can't believe anybody'd mind if I went in and peeked at the piano. Once, I heard a ragtime piece, another time a sad version of *Down in the Valley*, another what I think was the blues.

The saloon doors are the real kind, made of slatted wood and rounded curves and put in the center of the door frame so that the top and the bottom of the entrance stay open all the time. The doors swish behind me when I walk through, a great little whoosh of air that works just like a good book and spins me into the 1890s. That was an era where as a lady you got to wear fantastic dresses and parade around in hats. Either that, or you could pretend to be a boy and not raise any eyebrows when you walked into a drinking establishment.

The bar is dusky and smells of dust, and no one seems to be around. Just like I thought. But then I hear, behind the bar, a clink of glasses, and I guess that the bartender is down below, organizing for the night ahead. But aside from an old rancher asleep at the counter, there's not another soul, and I walk without a sound across waxed hardwood floors to the piano.

It sits upright at a right angle to the back wall of the stage area, the stage itself just a half-circle platform raised up a step from the rest of the bar. With his back to a corner, the piano man's side would be mostly to the audience. His front would be to his own piano and beyond that, the rest of the stage. I walk around the piano and go up to the shiny black bench in front of it. I lift the lid; I love the secretness of the storage space there. Inside, I look for musical scores, since I don't own any blues and the one folksong book is at home on my own piano. But here! Cool. I take out something called *South Side Piano: A Tribute to the Chicago Blues*. Underneath that is a book of gospel, and a *Folksongs of the American West*.

I grab the blues book and slide onto the seat. My legs dangle an inch or two off the floor. The book falls open along a break in its spine to something called *Rocket 88*. I put my fingers on the keys. The light's dim so I have to squint to read the score—c,b,a, I whisper, trying to match my voice with the keys. There aren't any chords, either; everything's rolling off, like a river.

I dare to play the first handful of notes.

"Hey!" The bartender jumps up, hitting his head.

Oops. I stop.

"Whaddareya doing, kid? Jeez." He puts down a tiny glass he's been polishing and comes out around the bar.

"I'm just playing," I say. "My mom's getting her hair cut now and I just wanted to—"

"You read music?"

The bartender looks like a combination of a cowboy and one of Dad's students.

"Yes."

"You play the blues?"

"That's why...that's why I wanted to come in here. 'Cause, see, I don't have any blues books at home, and I hear it coming out of here sometimes when I walk by on the street, and I like it and—"

"Let her play, Stoney," says a voice coming from the saloon doors. The voice sounds like tires crunching on gravel. Silhouetted against the light coming in from the street is a round, squat shape. I know, though, even before I can see his face, that he's the bum from the rail yard.

"Hey!" I say. Stoney shakes his head and goes back to the bar.

The bum lumbers like an old bull I used to see on the way to school. "Hay is for horses," he grumbles, but it sort of seems like he's smiling. "So you don't know the blues?"

"No. But I—"

"Close the damn book."

"What? But—"

"Close the book."

I don't like this, no notes in front of me.

"Okay," I say. "I closed it."

"Good. Now scoot over."

The fat man lowers himself onto the bench next to me. He smells like tobacco and a little bit like booze. Overall, it's a sweet smell and I like it.

"Close your eyes."

I close them.

"Now listen." And the old bum lets go into a rollicking blues number.

"Wow," I say, when he's all done. "What's that called?"

The bum opens the book back up.

"Rocket 88."

"The key to the blues is listening." I'm back again, the next

Saturday. Mom's at the grocery store.

"Where'd you learn them?" I ask.

He guffaws. "Young lady, I've been everywhere. I've worked for every damn railroad in this country. Picked up the blues in the Depression first, I guess, riding rail cars with all the others. A lot of them were black. We'd sit in the dark waiting for trains and they'd pull out these cheap guitars they'd bought from Sears or stole from their uncles or something, and they'd just sing all night."

"Oh," I say, quiet. What an amazing life.

"Do you ride rails anymore?"

He laughs. "How old do you think I am?"

I shrug.

He spreads his hands on the keyboards. "See, blues is just a matter of twelve riffs, over and over again, in different combinations—" He stops when he sees me staring at him. "What are you looking at?"

I know I'm blushing. "Nothing," I say. "How'd you end up here?"

"I was born here. Grew up out by Mancos. Why?"

"What's your name?"

"Oh for Chrissake. You ask too many cotton-pickin' questions, you know that? A man'd get killed asking questions like that on the rails." But he grins, as much as a gruff person like that can grin. "Name's Joe Peterman."

"Nice to meet you, Joe. My name's Sarah."

"Nice to meet you, Sarah," he says, like he's exasperated, and he offers me a big old hand that I take with my eyes bulging. Then he pulls it away like a shy bear and puts it back on the piano. "Jeez, kid, I'm not God," he mutters. But I know he's happy.

"Close my eyes?" I ask, as I see his fingers get ready.

"Close your eyes, gal."

Joe Peterman taps his foot and nods his body three times, and starts playing the sweetest, saddest blues song I think I've ever heard.

"I want to play the blues," I pout.

"Now, Sarah," says Mrs. Iverson. "We're working on etudes, not blues."

"I know. I hate etudes."

She blinks. I kind of blink myself. Where did that come from? I feel bad right away. What if Mrs. Iverson tells Mom? Says I asked to learn the blues and was rude about it? Mom will turn all purple about being rude and then say no to the blues with that flappy air she gets when she's going through territory she knows nothing about. And then she'll pull herself together, haughty, and give me the reason that blues are not acceptable. I imagine bugging her, not satisfied with that reason. Not acceptable for what? But if I keep bugging her Mom'll just turn me over to Dad, who will say, How can you learn the blues when you won't even master your etudes? No logic there either. God. And he's a scientist!

But there's no fighting it because there's nothing sane to fight. So I shut down the crazy connection they make between mastering etudes and moving on to the blues. Shut down even trying to ask for what I want from Mom to begin with. It'll just end up in—Dad's glassy blue eyes swim in front of me. I fumble quickly and open the etude book for Iverson. Iverson nods, smiling, and informs me as I stretch my hands as far as they will go that Chopin, who wrote the etudes, had exceptionally long fingers.

Ricky scowls at me when it's his turn. "Are you going to Trent's?"

"Yes. He's even meeting me out front."

Ricky strains his neck past Iverson's floaty see-through drapes and sees a boy, beige bandages wrapping his face and arms, sitting under a weak-looking maple. Ricky wrinkles his nose. "How can you stand to go near that freak? He looks like a sicko."

"Shut up."

"You shut up." And he pushes me a little as he moves past to Iverson, who waits at the piano, fiddling with the metronome.

Trent's mom has lemonade and cookies for us, but she's left a note on the table telling us to leave her alone for a little while because she's writing more on her next knitting book.

"Doesn't that bug you?" I ask, looking down at the note with a cookie in my hand.

"What bugs me?"

"That your mom says not to bug her?"

"No. It's good that she isn't over me all the time. When I first got home, Jeez. She was there all the time. My dad had to pull her away. Naw, if I need her, she'll come running."

If I need her, she'll come running.

"Oh," I say, my cookie gluey all of a sudden and sticking to the top of my mouth. I have trouble swallowing. I switch the subject. "Can I see your face?"

Trent shakes his head. "No. Taking this bandage off is too hard. You have to ruin it to get it off so the doctor does it. Then they put a new one on."

"Oh. Well, can I see your arm?"

"Okay." He pushes aside the elastic wrap holding the grafts in place, enough for me to see a swatch of forearm. I walk around the table to get a closer look.

"Ew. Doesn't it itch?"

"Yeah," he says, pushing the bandage back down too quickly.

"What did you do that for? I wasn't done looking."

Trent gets up and thrashes into the kitchen with his milk glass and cookie plate.

"You went 'ew.' Sorry I gross you out."

I stare at him. He stares back. The lump that started in my throat while I listened to Trent explain about his mom grows into a solid knot.

I didn't mean to upset him. If I upset people they'll, they'll... I pucker my mouth so I won't cry and whirl away from him toward the front door.

I bump right into Mrs. MacIntosh.

I stare at her the way I stared at Trent—hard, unmoving. I push the bangs up on my face. "Move," I say. I sound like I'm being strangled.

Mrs. MacIntosh gives way, and I fly out the door, a hundred thousand tears chasing me down the block.

"Hey, Ricky," I say, attempting to be friendly. I still feel lousy from what happened at Trent's.

"What?" We're out in the sideyard between our house and Mrs. Oodegaard's, lying on the grass. It's dusk, and dinner's almost ready.

"I want to learn the blues."

"You can't. I barely got ragtime past Iverson and Mom, and that was only 'cause it's so full of technique." Ricky is getting really good at ragtime.

"I went into the saloon at the Kittredge. This old guy started to teach me."

"You did what?" Ricky sits up.

"I went—"

"When?"

"Last Saturday. When I was supposed to be at the library when Mom—"

"I don't believe you."

"It's true."

"So what happened?"

"You know that old bum who hangs out at the rail yard? Well, he plays there."

"You weren't afraid of him?" Ricky looks at me a long time.

"No. I'm not."

"So he started teaching you?"

"Yeah, well, kind of. I—"

Ricky stands up suddenly, wiping the grass off his backside.

"What's the matter?" I ask.

"You can't be better than me at that. You just can't."

"Ricky, I'm not try—"

"You're always better than me at everything. You're Mom and Dad's favorite." Daggers form and shoot from his eyes. "Bitch," he curses. "Oh yes, little pussy lips," and he rubs his crotch obscenely. "Mommy and Daddy's favorite."

He stumbles away from me toward the house, but not before throwing me a look that reminds me of Dad.

For the second time that day, I have to keep from crying. I keep my head down, with my bangs covering my eyes, when I sneak past Ricky's room and into my own. There, I get out the paho I made for myself. I dream about playing blues around a campfire at Mesa Verde. I try to keep the image in focus. I even invent a great scene with a handsome Indian who loves me.

But it doesn't do any good. I have to fight like hell to keep Ricky's scowls from intruding. Trent's, too.

Mad mad, why is everybody so mad? I don't know. But the next Sunday morning, Ricky sets the back hillside on fire.

OURAY

I see him do it. He takes some foul-smelling red smoke out of a bottle and runs up below my crevice with it. Sarah goes after him, yelling, "You're not supposed to do that anywhere but the driveway!" That only makes him madder and he runs faster.

"Fuck you," he yells back at her, but she catches up to him at her oak house and tries to pull the bottle with the smoke away from him.

From where I lie it looks to me as if he gets an evil glint in his eye then, as if the minute that girl tries to stand up for herself, stop something, the rage of bad spirits tumbles down on her.

"Come on, Ricky," she whines. "If you set the mountain on fire Mom and Dad'll kill you." But I see her looking wildly around, at her makeshift broom, up at me. Most of all she wants him out of there. Out of the one place I know for sure now she feels can be a home.

"Fuck you. Leave me alone."

When she makes one more grab for the bottle he actually punches her. Pushes her down. I think he's younger, but not by much, and he's a little bigger. Great Spirit, if that were Paron I'd wring the sunlight out of him. On the ground, him puffing over her, the smoke drifting up, Sarah's got eyes full of terror, and then she does something curious and so wrong to me. She buckles in at her crotch. Hands first, then the protective fetal curl that men do when they've been kicked there. "Noooo!!!" she screams, and rolls away from him, rolls out into the old fallen oak leaves moldy from so many snows, and stands up well out of his way.

I start tilting again. Great Spirit, the world is off here. I shake my head as she backs off the hillside.

The world is off. Something about her position. That place on the ground. Paron under covers, hoping for safety? Something like that. That's where my head goes just looking at her, and I have to wince even as I want to save her.

The air's thick with harm. And just then I smell smoke of a woodsier sort, and the slight crackle of flames trying to take on a bed of leaves and sticks.

It isn't till the fire trucks come and a small circle of curious neighbors stands about that I see Mrs. Oodegaard again, off to the left in the Graves' side yard. In the daylight I can see that she's fatter than I remember, and gray.

She waddles back into what must be her own house, a small white cottage with a low stone wall dividing her yard from the Graves'. It hangs peripheral to my vision, hard for me to see over there for long without getting a headache, so I've never paid much attention. But she waddles back out again soon, this time with a cookie tin. I've lost Sarah but in following Mrs. Oodegaard I find her again. She's slumped on the grass, alone in the midst of a small crowd of people and hoses and red fire cars that look like Iron Horse cars without the tracks—I guess they're cars, because that's what they called smaller ones like these when I was haunting—her legs crossed and her head buried in her hands. Oodegaard opens the tin, stoops down, and offers her whatever's in it.

Sarah looks up. It's a little far, I can't really read her expression, but to me her body shuffles back a bit. As if she's scared of Oodegaard. Why? And where is Lars? Is Lars dead? With all the people around come out of the woods for the fire, I would think he might be there. But I don't see him.

Mrs. Oodegaard apparently says something to Sarah that startles her, but works, because Sarah shyly takes a cookie. *Good for you, Mrs. O, good for you.* Ricky's held hostage by his father's hands firmly on his shoulders, standing next to a fireman and sobbing out what I can only imagine is some kind of apology.

The fire's out quickly; what's left is smoke. The firemen roll up their hoses and Sarah takes another cookie. Lars still does not appear. When Mrs. Oodegaard retreats to her house, and beyond my point of view, I feel, for the first time in ages, the compulsion to spirit-walk. Not to haunt, but to find out what happened. What happened to Lars, and what rotten thing is happening to Sarah, to these children, right under my lousy nose.

Mothers

When I offer her the cookie and she recoils, I say to her, "Don't worry. I didn't kill Lars," and it seems to be just the right thing. Because even though Sarah blushes, she also starts to speak.

"How did you know?" she asks.

"That you were afraid of me because of Lars?" I stick the cookie tin her way again and she takes one this time. "Lord, my dear. I haven't lived this long for nothing. Unless, of course, there's some other reason why you wouldn't like me?"

Sarah breaks the cookie in half, hiding behind her bangs. "No," she mumbles. She seems ashamed now.

"It's all right," I say. "I've gotten used to people being afraid." The wind shifts and brings the smell of damp smoke to my nose. I stoop down next to her, heavy as I am. "Do you want to tell me about the fire?"

Sarah's silent a minute, ducking down further under her bangs. I sigh, thinking I've lost her again. Then she says, "He almost burned down my house up there."

"House?"

"My *Little House on the Prairie* house."

I laugh. "Is that what you do up there, all dressed up?"

Sarah flushes.

"It's all right, dear. I used to be a Pioneer Girl once. I lived a lot like Mrs. Wilder."

Her eyelids go up. "You did?"

"Yes. I did." And I tell her all about it, about the wide plains of western Nebraska, the hard winters. I mention the time the cow gave birth on the front stoop. I tell her how wind sounds through tall grass, and what it's like to be able to see in all directions. I tell her about pretty little snakes, and blue birds' eggs nested in the dirt. I tell her how far I walked to school, and how neatly the homestead sections were gridded off.

Sarah listens, her arms hugging her knees, jeans and sneakers a little muddy from spring snowmelt. By the time I'm done talking, the firemen have left, and even Sarah's father and brother have gone back inside. It's late afternoon now, and Sarah looks tired.

"You better go," I say.

But Sarah lingers, as if making up her mind about something. "Can I have another cookie?" she asks.

"Certainly." I hand her the tin.

"Mrs. Oodegaard?"

"Hmmm?"

"I see you up at night sometimes."

My arm stops midway in returning the cookie tin to my side. "You do?"

"Yes."

"Well," I swallow, "I see a light over at your place, too, upon occasion."

"You do?" I can practically feel Sarah's face burn, and she won't look in my direction.

"Yes. In the basement."

The red in her face increases but her eyes begin to glaze over. "Oh, well, yeah," she says. "Sometimes my dad can't sleep, I guess." Sarah looks away abruptly and up toward the hillside.

"Tell you a secret," she says.

"What?" I ask.

"I know where Chief Ouray is buried."

I don't know what I expected, but it isn't this. I almost drop the cookie tin. "Where? Up there?" I point to the hill. My heart is pounding. You'd think it was Lars she found.

Sarah giggles, a little nervous now. "Not saying," she says. "Maybe next time." And she pouts off, wiping her backside free of grass.

I understand. *Next* time. I'm surprised how disappointed I feel.

SARAH

Next Wednesday I go to Trent's, as usual. On the inside of my notebook I've got the Four Corners, and this time I have a person for each state. Mrs. MacIntosh is for New Mexico, because my teacher from Taos told us the word for spider in her village was the same as for weaver *(La Arana)* and because Mrs. MacIntosh just went to Taos to buy wool. Mrs. Oodegaard is for Colorado, of course, because she's lived here so long. Both Mrs. MacIntosh and Mrs. Oodegaard have little questions next to their names, but the question next to Ouray is long gone. I talk to him almost every day now.

Trent and I play fine until I open my notebook to get a piece of paper and the fire-bombing story from the Denver *Post* flies out. I grab for it, but not before Trent sees the headline. Our eyes meet and for a split second I feel totally confused. I really want to talk about the story, but I don't want to upset him. I still feel bad about the day when I went "Ewww" over his arm, and Mrs. MacIntosh preached to me later not to ask to see Trent's burned places again. My ears were on fire when she talked to me like that; *of course* I wouldn't ask again. I didn't ever want to lose someone over my own stupid mistakes.

"What is that?" Trent asks.

"Nothing."

"Come on, let me see." He reaches for it, lunging with his left arm.

"NO. Trent—" But he's got a piece, and the article starts to tear. I give it up before it all falls apart. "Now look what you've done!"

"Sorry," he pouts, but I can tell he doesn't mean it, and he lays the article flat on the floor, smoothing the torn pieces back together so he can read it.

"I want it back, Trent." I try to keep my voice from choking, but I'm not very successful.

He looks up at me with sharp eyes, beady like the eagles I've seen at zoos and even on fence posts in the wintertime. "Why does this matter so much to you? Why are you reading stories about burning all the time?" He's practically hollering at me now. "What's wrong with you?"

What's wrong with me. Always what's wrong with me. "Trent, see— I just want to know how they escaped. How they got out of there."

"Who?"

"The two boys in the article. They were the only ones who escaped, see—"

My idea of sharing is not working. Trent's eyes go hard and stare at me.

I swallow.

"MO-OM!" He screams, and breaks the horrible held-breath silence of the second before.

Footsteps on carpet, hurried. Door opening. The legs of Trent's mom, blue jeans, looming. "What is it, honey?"

But Trent is sobbing on the floor, flailing at me with his one good arm. Hate rolls out of his eyes in waves and hits me. "I didn't escape, Sarah! Get it? I didn't escape!" He wads the newspaper article up furiously and tosses it at me.

"Sarah, honey, let's go," says Mrs. MacIntosh. She extends her hand and I take it, but not before reaching for the ball of newspaper and my notebook.

Out in the hallway, Mrs. MacIntosh says, "Stay here a minute while I go calm Trent down."

First Dad, then Ricky, now Trent. Boys who hate me. What did I ever do? I don't even try to hear what Trent's mom and Trent are saying, all muffled, through the door to Trent's bedroom. I don't even look at the carpet at my feet. It's all I can do not to plaster myself on the ceiling the way I do with Dad.

Mrs. MacIntosh comes out of the bedroom. She puts her arm

around me and walks me to the front door.

"Sarah," she starts, playing with the buttons on her sweater and not looking at me. Uh-oh. I've never seen Mrs. MacIntosh not be able to tell me something. My stomach twists and my ears shut down in preparation.

"Sarah, I think it's best if you and Trent didn't see each other for a while."

My ears are underwater. Her words create the ocean. Everything becomes muffled—Mrs. MacIntosh's voice, the hum of the refrigerator, the birds chirping outside.

"Sarah? Did you hear me? It's just that—look, honey," and she squats down and takes my hands, tries to find my eyes under my bangs. I just keep my hands limp the way I do with my own mom when she tries to get all kissy-face, and I won't look up. But Mrs. MacIntosh goes on. "For him to get better, not just physically, but psychologically, having his family support him is the best thing. Especially in the first year. It's only been six months since the accident. Can you understand that?"

But all I can think is that I'm all alone now, really. I've blown it. I've lost another mother. Another mother hates me now. Everybody hates me. *Throw her out. Don't let her in here.*

I don't respond to Mrs. MacIntosh except to pull my hands out from hers. A horrible urge to leave, like a body-long itch, crawls all over me. I want to leap out of my skin. I can't stand to be myself that much. *It's just like after Daddy.* Or when Mommy blows up at me after being friendly. *Attack, attack. Watch your back.*

I don't even have any strength to watch my back, though. Mrs. MacIntosh is the last straw. My eyes feel dead, so does my heart. They both go inward inward inward.

"Sarah?"

I won't recognize. All I hear are Trent's words, flashing like a neon sign in the middle of the night out in the desert: *Don't you get it Sarah? I didn't escape.* And of course I feel like screaming, *I didn't either. I still haven't. At least people believe you.*

No one believes me; I don't have any scars you can see the way he does. Maybe Down There, but I wouldn't let anyone near there anyway and Down There is usually covered by clothes.

I curl in on myself, like a snail. I walk out of the MacIntosh's house without even being able to move my lips to say goodbye.

Do what you want. Doesn't matter.

He's fucking me. No light even needed, just three a.m. and he's fucking me. *Why aren't I on the ceiling yet?* He's got me from behind and he has his big dick— Like a dog. Like Beowulf and Yuma that one time. Exactly like that. He tried this when I was small but he only got so far in because I was too little. But now. I'm stretched, so stretched, stretched stretched stretched and a burning feeling when he first got as far in as he has. He even has me by the hair, caveman style.

Almost eleven. I am almost eleven. I'm crying now, I can actually feel myself crying, and I let my sobs match with his jabbing so that he won't figure that out. He'll just do it harder if he finds out that I'm crying. It excites him. When I said no—I actually said no this time, almost eleven and a little taller and after Mrs. MacIntosh—I don't know, something is just giving up hope so it doesn't matter anymore what I say—he boxed my left ear, smacked my skull. I couldn't believe it. Until then he always whined, or was silent, scientist silent. But now, now the fire's up another notch and if I don't—if I don't—

Find something sexy in this.

He wants me. That's it. *He's always saying how sexy this all is.* Yeah. *He wants me so bad he'll hit me for it.* Yeah. In fact—did he say that? Hard to tell with the sea rushing out of my ears, the left one throbbing. Hard to tell with my whole body back to crouching like a gargoyle on the light fixture on the ceiling, then falling off again. Hard to tell.

I feel old. Beyond almost eleven. Like a whore woman.

He's fucking me. Three a.m.

Find something sexy. He wants me, that's it.

Yeah. Fuck her more.

BARBARA

Vacancy. Three a.m., and I cannot escape the look in Sarah's eyes. The look comes to me in dreams, accompanied by one of the mummies I saw once when younger, before they'd taken them off display at Mesa Verde. The mummy in my dream is not, strangely, hard to look at. There is a maternal kindness about her that I find both comforting and familiar, for the mummy reminds me of myself on better days.

Which makes me feel as if I've betrayed that part of me that is a good mother.

Sarah's face, in the last, stark moments of her existence in my house, bore a recognizable look, a look I'd seen before. It was the look of Trent the week after the scalding accident. It bore an uncanny resemblance to myself after my father's death when I was twelve. I used to stare and stare at myself in the mirror and see only eyes, a skull sheathed tightly in skin, a kind of ghastly shriek waiting to emit but never, never, doing so. Yes. I knew that look.

In the heavy, wee hours, then, the mummy wakes me up with Sarah, holding the back of Sarah's head in a pecan-colored craw and presenting her to me as if to say, in a demeanor more serious than I have ever known (with the exception of Paul Carson on the day of Trent's accident), *Look.*

I go to the kitchen for a cup of hot cocoa. My hair's growing out and I've plaited it into a frizzy, short braid, but strands of it still reach out and tickle my nose. I blow them away gently, even though they just resettle. I don't turn on a light because moonlight shafts in through the sliding glass door of the dining area, as well as the window over the kitchen sink, and that is enough. I need no surprises tonight, no harsh lights, no abrupt transitions. I need to glide around in the shadows, probing in the transitional places. I need to stay in the spot between what I know and don't know, the crack where the mummy falls in through time and logic.

What kind of mother am I? The moonlight catches the smoky curls of steam off of my cup of cocoa. I still wince a little at steam, but my hands wrap around the mug gratefully, feeling cold. In the face of my helplessness—the worst feeling I've ever had to experience, and one I thought I would never revisit after my father died—I've done everything since Trent has come home to try and make things better. I've buffered him against the stunned stares of the few classmates who visited at first, then against the fact that no one visited. I've lectured Brandon time and again to be kind to his brother, while at the same time trying to understand my younger boy's fears that he would be overlooked, abandoned in the face of the monstrosity of Trent's tragedy. I've tried to pull my family back into the calm configuration it lay in before the accident, a configuration I built for myself on the grief of my father's fate, his lanky body crushed between Jeep and rock, metal and granite. But there are some scars that may last as long as the ones on Trent.

Sarah came as such a relief. I've marveled at that little girl's courage. When everyone else would take one look at Trent and go away, Sarah stayed. In fact, it seems Sarah has the opposite problem; she's more obsessed than scared.

I shake my head. No, obsessed is too unfair. For Sarah's developed a genuine friendship with Trent. She doesn't come over just to look at his wounds. She wants to see, yes, but that isn't what, in the main, drives her to prefer Trent's company. It might have been at first, but not now. There have been too many times of walking past Trent's room and hearing laughter, too many times when I've seen Sarah come hotly to Trent's defense, usually in the face of some transgression of Brandon's. And lastly, I've seen tenderness, a stark compassion that is jarring in someone so young. Sarah will arrange pillows for Trent without ever making him feel like an imbecile; she'll ask him if he's cold or hot precisely when he is, in fact, cold or hot. She'll walk slowly, at his pace, with him. She doesn't insist that he become normal, heal faster, get over it. She wants him better, but she accepts what he is.

Tears pool in me. Maybe it's Trent who needs a little lecture, not Sarah. Maybe Trent needs to get over his sensitivities. It has helped since he's gone back to school. The kids have stopped gawking and a few have even bothered to play with him a little. But no one comes close to Sarah. No one.

SARAH

No one. It's morning and there's no one. I don't know how I get back up to my room. I never do. All I know is that when it's all over I am naked and bleeding and sore and cold in the basement, and that Mom never comes. That's all I know.

That stupid goose tried to flutter on the window again but I opened the window and told it to go the hell away. I also crossed out Mrs. MacIntosh from my Four Corners map.

No one. Not even Mrs. MacIntosh. Out in the kitchen, toast and juice I don't want. *I'm sick I'm sick I'm sick. It's all my fault. If it weren't WHY wouldn't she come get me?* Stab stab stab take the butter knife—

"Sarah! What are you doing?" The shocked emu-face of her staring down at me, jerking the butter knife out of my hand. "What are you doing? Are you all right, honey?"

Mom really looks at me, head-on, for the first time in my whole life. I can't believe it.

Am I all right? Do I look like it? My eyes feel like the sockets of a skull, like Ouray's. My entire face must look like that, or like the skulls Leakey finds in the African desert. I shake my head, and drop my eyes behind my bangs. *Don't see me.*

"What's the matter?"

I don't answer.

Mom stands up, kind of nervous. "I wish you'd tell me," she says, in that voice that's half real concern and half sour grapes at not being allowed to know everything. Mom doesn't notice much unless she can get something out of it. "Well," she sighs, "if nothing's really wrong, go get ready for school."

Get ready for school? A broken down feeling soaks my bones like kerosene on Dad's rags. How can I make her see? But then if she does see...?

I go to the shower. Lock the door. Shower. Shower. Scald. Scald like Trent. *That's what you deserve, stupid girl.* Arm in, but I can't stand it. Shrieks. Mom comes running.

"Sarah? Open up!"

I unlock. I face Mom with a towel clinging around my body. *No way can she see me naked. Not her. She'll hate me. She'll invade. She'll kill me.* But tears stream down my face, I can't help it, and I'm shaking.

"Sarah, honey, what is it? You'll catch a cold."

"I threw up." Which is true. This morning at six a.m. Now the barfy feeling happens again. Daddy's left for work, though; maybe it'll be safe to stay home. Mom will just shut herself in her room but she might bring me drinks.

Mom puts a hand to my forehead. I let her even though I don't like her touching me. *You can't fake like you care now.* "No fever. But if you want to stay home, you can."

Relief. Just for a second, though. Now an entire day with nothing to do stretches a zillion miles in front of me. I think about crawling back in bed and—what? Caving in on that horrible pain? Moping about the way I seem to drive away even the most loving people? *Not even my own mother wants to save me. Not even Mrs. MacIntosh.* Just thinking about it makes me want to hurt myself again.

But to go to school seems like too much. People will know. Will see how awful I am. Which is worse? To stay home and mope, or go to school? Mom looks at me, waiting for an answer.

I slump. My arm is starting to sting from the scald.

"I'll stay home," I say.

Mom pecks my cheek and smiles. "Okay. I'll get you some 7-UP and comic books later, how's that?"

"Okay." It's a glimmer. It gives me a little courage.

"Mom?" I ask.

"Yes?"

"What do you think about what happened to Trent?"

Mom shudders. "I can't even talk about it."

Just like I thought, but it's still like a metal door slamming shut for good. It rings and rings. *She can't talk about anything.*

As soon as Mom leaves, I point myself over the toilet and throw up for the second time that morning.

I curl up under my sheets and play house with Miss Mouse, a stuffed mouse my artist godmother Rachel made me. Miss Mouse wears a frock with a floral print apron, and a bonnet. I also have two baby mice, and some doll furniture. I sing a little to myself, setting up a living room on the smooth bottom sheet, the top sheet and blankets over my head to make a tent. I haven't played Miss Mouse in a long time.

All goes just fine for a while. Miss Mouse sweeps, the child mice lie in their cradle, Miss Mouse is visited by Mr. Badger (a suitor), like in Beatrix Potter. Mr. Badger stays for tea. They talk about little things. Trifles. The weather. Then it gets awkward, silent. *What next?* Panic.

Have to keep the man all to yourself. Doesn't matter if you're smart and have lots of degrees and can teach and Mr. Badger's an idiot. Have to keep Mr. Badger.

But then the children mice break in. "Mommy, Mommy. Can we go out and play?" They tug at her skirts.

"Did you clean your room? Do your homework?" Miss Mouse growls at them, fierce. They're distracting Miss Mouse from entertaining.

The little mice begin to cower. "Yes, Mommy. Yes."

"Bullshit!" A Ricky-like explosion. "You did NOT! Bad mice. Bad children!" WHAM. A toy broom comes down. Wham! Wham! Wham! Beating little stuffed mice into the sheets.

"Bad children." Tears and mucus slide all over my face, a volcano in me making each blow. Furniture sails toward the sky, the sheets wrinkle, Mr. Badger bounces to the floor. The broom isn't enough, so I start beating the mice with the cradle. "Bad Bad BAD!"

The cradle acts like a hatchet, the hard wood cutting into the stuffed animal softness of the mice.

"Bad…bad…" But the fight is going out of me. My voice fades. Then I see that stuffing has leaked out of one of the little mice.

I pick up the hurt mouse. Stroke it. "Ohhhh…I am so sorry," I say. I shove all the other toys to the floor. I fall and sob into my pillow, the little mouse between my fingers. I can feel the soft cloth in my hands, and the place where the stuffing is coming out. I plug my thumb into the hole. Could be such a lovely mouse…don't kill…don't go yet…save yourself…it's a good mouse, really, pretty mouse… I'll sew you up later, promise…

I start to fall asleep. The mouse cloth gets softer and softer, till I dream I am holding a goose.

BARBARA

I wake up with two days of resolve pouring into my bones like plaster into a mold. Two days since I told Sarah to back off, and then Trent coming home to say Sarah wasn't at school yesterday. A draining feeling in the gut at that; and so this morning, my stiffening determination.

Sarah better be there today because I plan to meet her. I imagine intercepting her on her way to the long line of buses parked and waiting for their passengers in front of the school. I don't know which bus Sarah takes, but I tell myself it doesn't matter—the path from the school building to the buses is the same. I ignore the fact that there will be a hundred other children, running and shouting, in that direction. Sarah sticks out in my mind like a candle flame, a unique light

I will see as if from on high, as if I were given the vision of the peaks, who guard the known world of the school by defining its perimeter, by standing, impassive, day after day after day, their snowy beauty a strange assurance. I know; I grew up with those peaks; La Plata is my childhood home as well. I know exactly what it means to be young and alive in that world, to count elk in the meadows in winter, to listen to the river rattle and rush in spring, to watch as the snow melts and the rocks lining the roadsides glisten with sudden water. But then I start tearing up because my father was responsible for me knowing that world, for showing me without ever opening his mouth where to go for refuge when people let you down. Even when I was mad at him, I went where he had given me permission to go—to the rocky peaks, the talking river, the eerie but familiar sound of willows speaking in the wind.

Dear Dad, I became a hawk once, and danced right along the edge where grass meets sky. And I would talk to the willow and the willow would listen. And when the deer or otter intruded, suddenly, I'd be so happy I couldn't speak. Dear Dad. Dear God, Dad. There is so much left to tell you. Every year there is so much left—

I have to stop this. I have to remember all that beauty without falling somewhere unreal and full of fantastical, hopeless hope. I shake myself, smile sadly, and think that between now and this afternoon I should revisit my childhood haunts, my favorite, secret places nestled under brambles or perched high on rocks overlooking the town. But then the phone rings, and it's the school nurse.

"Mrs. MacIntosh? Your boy Trent here is upset and says he wants to go home. Says he's sick but he doesn't have a fever—"

"Let me talk to him."

The phone transfers hands and Trent's sniffly voice comes on. I cradle the phone. "Trent? What is it?"

Sniff. Hand wiping nose, I can hear it. "Mom, Sarah won't play with me."

"What do you mean, honey?"

"She ran a hundred miles away from me this morning at recess. She's never done that."

"Well, you know I told her it might be good if she didn't come over to the house for a while." But as I'm saying this, I realize I told Sarah to stay away in general. Sarah's retracted eyes come back to me, and I make a face.

Trent tries to talk through a clogged voice. "Well, I guess she thought you meant at school too. To stay away, I mean."

Silence. I am thinking.

"Mom?"

"Umm?"

"Don't tell her that again. I mean, tell her to come back."

"You mean that?" I ask. "You've been awfully touchy, Trent. I was trying to make a decision based on what's best for you. But now I think maybe you were a little sensitive. Sarah…" I stop, intake of breath suspended at the thought that comes into my mind… "Sarah loves you, I think, Trent."

Silence again. Sniffles. A strained, tight voice, caught in wires of emotion and mucus. "I love her too, Mom. Get her back."

Phone line dead. I look at the receiver, amazed. Songs break out inside. *I've done something right. My little boy can love again.*

I don't wait for three o'clock. I drive right over to the school, pull Trent out of class, and by deliberately exuding an overdone charm and motherly air of confidence, manage to extract Sarah from her classroom as well. Sarah looks at both of us, stunned. The school hallway is vacant and echoey, light coming in from the end doors and illuminating the brick. Caught off guard, Sarah's expression flickers in and out between what looks to me like eager hope and the defensive urge to extinguish herself.

I have to work fast. "Trent has something he wants to say to you." I kneel to my son. *Sotto voce*, gently prodding. "Go on, honey. Tell her what you told me on the phone earlier."

"That I love her?" Trent whispers back. I nod. I see that his eyes are wild with terror. "No *way*," he hisses. But I hold his gaze.

Trent sucks in a large bite of air and faces Sarah. The two children stare at each other. "Sarah…," he stammers. I nudge him. Trent's chin trembles with words he cannot muster. "Sss-Sar…" And before he can stop he bursts into tears and throws his arms—elastic encased, wincing in their delicacy—around his friend. They half hug her, half hit her, he's so mad and happy.

I watch as Sarah's face retreats from all defense. From over Trent's shoulder her eyes bug out and she gawks at me with complete surprise. A blush blossoms, bright red, all over her cheeks.

I can't hide my grin. I usually hate pushy mothers, but pushing Trent just now worked. Wicked thoughts ply my mind.

"Let's ditch," I say. My eyes narrow like a cat's. If I had a tail, it would twitch.

"Mom!" Trent lets go of Sarah and turns back around.

"Well?"

"Where would we go?"

"Somewhere I went when I was little. Come on. I'll get us some ice cream."

Trent looks at Sarah. "Can you? She'll get you back to the bus in time, I promise."

"I guess so." Sarah still looks floored. "Um, let me tell Ricky."

"Okay."

So we find Ricky, and tell him, and skip out of the school on the mesa. We go down the hill to Safeway and buy ice cream, where we run into Madeleine Oodegaard. I find out she and Sarah are neighbors. Sarah seems surprised at this but I am too happy to linger. I rustle my bag full of ice cream and spoons and cups and cross them over the train tracks and the bridge. We sit on the east side of the river. I tell them how I grew up three blocks from here, and how I came here when I was upset. Trent nestles in my arms, and though I've asked Sarah if she'd like to join us, Sarah sits shyly, a little apart. After a while, we stop talking. The willows rustle. I don't tell them to listen because I know they already are. They are children. I close my eyes into this sweetness, while up the river a remnant crew of snow geese murmurs excitedly and the river wafts the news to the peaks, who've been sleeping on updrafts of cool April air.

Savants

Damn but here's *another* set of skirts. A heap of huffing and puffing. The sun high, warm day. Sarah's not around, and the ground must be soggy because I see mud on the huffer's shoes. I hear her coming, have heard the huffing and puffing for a while now, as if she were looking for something. Combing the hillside the way ants do. And the skirts walk right by me the first time. They go a few steps past me, then stop. She smells like lilacs again.

She stops, then turns back toward me. I'm busy trying to organize my bones. Trying to tie together all the little chips of my spirit that have gotten lazy and fallen apart in the crevice. I don't want to meet her as a skeleton. I need to be more awake than that. I need to ask her, up front, about Lars.

But she finds me first. "Ooh," she says, hand reaching toward my skull but then backing off as if I were a rattlesnake. Sarah never backs off. I'm breathing hard. Harder. Come on come on...

"Ouray?" she says.

"Y-ye-yes!"

And I worm out of my skeleton, golden and fringed, to stand next to her on the slope in front of my grave.

She's blinking rapidly. "Mrs. Oode—" I start, not knowing if she'll even be open to seeing me.

"Good heavens!" she says, her hand grabbing her chest. "You scared me."

She squints at me closer. Then she colors. "Oooh my. You really *are* Chief Ouray."

My old rage at the Oodegaard lack of fear revisits me for a second, like lightning. But then I remember that I'm not here to haunt, even though it dawns on me that talking to white people without anger or rage is something new for me. Even when I met President Grant, I kept my anger. I felt like a buffalo then, pawing the ground. There, it was powerful, served me well. It was anger, not rage. Anger came from a centered place, a powerful place. Rage was the emotion of victims, of powerless people. Of cornered mountain lions with no way out. But I'm not here to be angry or to snarl. I'm here to make amends.

"How do you know who I am?" I ask.

"Oh, Lars told me all about you. And the neighbor girl did some, too. And every time I hold an arrowhead I found out back, I get a sense of you."

"What'd Lars say?"

Mrs. Oodegaard's mouth works to find words. Up close her face is pillowed in lines and loose skin. "Lars was—Lars saw the world a little differently than most people. He was always magical. He saw God in everything. He had—he had bouts. Bouts of highs and lows. So when he told me about you, I wasn't that surprised."

"You talk about him as if he's not living."

"He isn't."

"When did he die?"

"Five years ago."

She turns her head, her face turned down with sorrow.

"I'm sorry," I say. "Was it…hard?"

Her eyes swoop to meet mine. They blaze oddly. Her irises have become so blue they look black, black in a sky of pale skin and white hair. Like a lake that's too deep. All of what she needs to say comes together in those dark pupils. Then she utters, her voice just the scratch of a squirrel, "He hung himself in the basement."

I sink. Dismay bleeds through me. *It must be me.* Lars must have killed himself, finally, because of my behavior. It doesn't matter that it was so many summers ago; what matters is that I nearly drove him to it once and who's to say it didn't rot inside all along, that Lars didn't carry it with him until one day...?

Just look how long I've been carrying things. Just look. "Aeiie, shit," I say, the last of my dignity going and the memory of the fiddler ghost's story hanging over me. Words Kit Carson told me drunk, over a campfire, come back to me. Cuss words, he said, laughing. Like *pendejo* or *puta, chinga tu madre*. In the Spanish of your childhood, remember, hombre?

I remember. And I use them now, in English; only I am not laughing.

MADDY

Sweetness, my sweetness, I loved you since you were ten. Out on that Nebraska plain, the schoolhouse perched on the highest hill, little boys and little girls from all the nearby homesteads walking there through the crisp morning light and the waving oceans of grass. I met him because we were both hiding things under the steps of the schoolhouse—him milkweed pods, locust husks, bee wings; me bluebird feathers, reddish agates, rabbit tails left over from a coyote's lunch. I hadn't thought much of the pile in the opposite corner, had assumed it was just the slow accumulation of nature's goodies, when he appeared as a silhouette on the other side of the steps, crouching down with the perfect yellow carcass of a monarch butterfly pinched between his fingers. He was singing softly to himself, laying the carcass carefully next to the locust shell. I stopped, hand frozen over the smooth, safe feeling of the agate I'd been grasping. In an unsteady squat, I found myself tottering. As I fought to stay still the sound of leather boot scraping gravel reached Lars' ears. His head lifted swiftly in the direction of the noise. I couldn't see his face in the dusk under the stairs and I guessed he couldn't see mine.

We both stood up at the same time, urgently in need of sunlight to identify the betrayer. A little boy met a little girl. We stared at each other without a word over the mound of steps, utterly still, the way rabbits freeze when in danger. We were both breathing furiously. We both, without a sound, issued an appeal to the other. *Don't tell anyone, and don't touch my stuff.*

It was a promise we managed to keep.

Lars' family lived two miles from the schoolhouse in the opposite direction from where I lived. His father was a taciturn man with classic Scandinavian cheekbones, strawberry blonde hair, and the complete conviction that Armageddon would come any day. He went from brand-name Lutheran to some sort of Seventh Day Adventist after hearing a child evangelist preach at the county fair one year. It did appear to suit him better, in that he possessed not an ounce of extravagance and seemed to thrive on leanness. Good years were harder on him than bad years—in good years the embarrassment of riches caught him out cold; he bought new clothes for his children and then told them to wear them out a bit around the farm before putting them on in public; in a rare fit of capitalistic sentiment (no doubt borne out of genuine need), he bought a Model A and then hid it until he'd gotten it good and muddy and scratched up. When my mother handed him a solid slab of venison one year, he colored visibly—both because my mother had always struck him as extravagant (she was prone to hats and bought books) and because the slab of meat seemed to provide too much surplus at one time. My mother smiled graciously at his stunned countenance and hustled me away from the Oodegaard front door. "Heavens, I hope his son is more fun than he is," she whispered. It was my turn to color then; I was sixteen and at that moment I realized my mother's gesture of venison was done because she knew I cared for Lars.

I don't know where Lars' collecting habits developed, though after knowing him as long as I have I believe they were a way of capturing lushness in a world that prohibited it. When the bad years came, and they started to come in droves right around the time of the Great War, his father relished it. Armageddon must be close and they would all go to heaven. But for Lars, Armageddon was Armageddon, terrifying and silly as something to put one's faith in. I know he fell in love with the earth as a baby and never got over it. The earth teemed with interesting things—ants and bees and coyote yips and nighthawk swoops. But because the only thing allowed to him was a belief in Jesus, Lars interpreted his great love as love of Him, and he never imagined he might love the world of its own right until we moved here. Funny how if you twist Christianity enough you end up so detached as that. Of course, my mother'd argue that love is Love, and Love is God, and God is indeed in all the ant nests and owl hoots if you can just be present enough to transcend into that. And Lars was. All the time. He was prescient. He could smell a thunderstorm miles off. Hear cattle long before others could. Find arrowheads and fossils better than anyone. And when his hands graced my back, finally, when we were teenagers and young love truly began to sprout, I practically fainted from the thought that his fingertips were three times as sensitive as anyone else's. I imagined him touching every nerve ending, each sighing muscle. There was no going back after that.

Of course, his father tried. Not only was he dismayed that his son had chosen the progeny of my frivolous mother, but that he had, as he'd hit his late teens, rejected the Seventh Day Adventist tradition. Lars didn't reject Jesus—that was too big a task—but he stalked off to the Lutheran church my family attended, and applied for a scholarship to seminary behind his father's back. When he got it, he found his father at the schoolhouse listening to government extension agents telling the farmers to plant shelter belts around their farms. The farmers had all tried that, years ago, to no avail. But the extension agents, East Coast-educated and dressed to the nines in wingtips and ties, didn't seem to know this. They lectured again and again on subjects everyone else already knew about, as if it were the homesteaders' fault that the soil was drying up and the rains didn't come. So Karl Oodegaard was not in the best of moods. Lars knew this but didn't care. He sidled up to him (I know because I sat a row back and five seats over, my breath held), showed him the letter announcing the award, and left before his father's face exploded. I have never seen a man turn so beet red in all my life. After the lecture, Karl cornered me in the yard, fingers digging into my elbow.

"This is your fault, young lady. All your fault." And he stalked off into the dying sun toward his ailing Model A, mouth drawn permanently closed this time. He never really opened his homestead up to anybody again.

Lars wept openly when his father died. We'd been in this house half a dozen years. He'd sent him money, always feeling that his father had neither the will nor the right piece of land to really make a living. When the letter came, saying he'd been found in his house, a good week into being dead, Lars crumbled. "There was never anything I could do," he cried. "And I tried so hard…"

Lars had been the last child by ten years. His mother died when he was five. So he might as well have been an only child, and certainly the only sibling to live with his father (a changed man) after his mother's death. The others couldn't understand Lars' particular misery. They all thought it was sad how their father died, but hadn't lived the sadness leading up to it.

Lars had. Lars, of the sensitive senses, of the intense mood swings, of transcendent clairvoyance. My Lars.

OURAY

"So I haunted a man who should have been a shaman."

"What?" Mrs. Oodegaard steeps tea by dangling a bag full of it up and down in her drinking cup. I've been offered some, but I tell her ghosts don't drink. We're in her yellow kitchen, made yellower by the fact that it's pitch dark outside and brightly lit inside. It's two a.m.

"Those things you talk about—his abilities," I continue. "In our tribe, he would have been chosen at an early age, and apprenticed to a shaman. You know, a medicine man. People with his gifts can be great healers."

For some reason tears show up in Mrs. Oodegaard's eyes. She holds them in by biting her lip. "Thank you," she says.

"What for?"

Mrs. Oodegaard sits down at a small yellow kitchen table, shiny legs and smooth top made out of a material I don't know anything about. She puts her head tiredly in one of her hands, the tea steaming in the other. "All my life," she says, "all my life I have wondered if I were not insane to love this man. He could be extraordinarily difficult. You've seen his moods. The craziness was almost worse than the depression. I carried my family through all of them. I carried my family when he couldn't. Sometimes I hated that. It was very hard…"

"But you loved him."

She looks up at me. "Oh yes. No one understood the payback from living with someone like that. There was always passion. Always a deep, deep river of feeling. As long as I didn't let my resentments get in the way, there were streams of things coursing between us, all the time. My life has been made immeasurably richer."

She sips the tea but her hands shake a little. I find my own heart quivering, the way your arm does when you are little and first trying to hold steady the drawn string of your bow. The first tears I've ever felt for a white person form in the underground spaces behind my eyes. Chipeta floats by, my long-lost beloved wife. She could be tough too, sometimes, though not like Lars. But I know about the things that can course between two people who love each other. They are like creeks meeting and dividing and meeting again.

"You're a brave woman," I say, swallowing.

"You really think so?"

"Oh yes. Yes, I do."

Llorona

SARAH

Mrs. Oodegaard was out turning over her flower bed this morning when me and Ricky showed up to wait for the bus, and she actually waved at me. I waved back. Now, sitting in class listening to Mrs. Lovato correct spelling tests out loud, I'm all warm with that wave, and with Mrs. MacIntosh, and with the bright green willows sprouting their leaves down by the river. If I don't watch it my head'll float right to the peaks, making everything a fairy tale. When I open up my notebook, I write Mrs. MacIntosh's name back in the state of New Mexico.

"Local Traditions time, class," Mrs. Lovato says, and some of the boys start groaning. But I sit up. I love this. Twice a week we do Local Traditions. This is where I first learned about Ouray. Mrs. Lovato started Local Traditions at the first of the year by talking about herself, and said her family had been in southern Colorado and northern New Mexico for nearly four hundred years. Mostly east of La Plata, in the big valley over Mouache pass, but her branch settled La Plata because of two brothers who wanted to mine.

I'm in love with the four hundred years part. I imagine Mrs. Lovato's family having these really long roots, that dangle and weave together forever underground. Almost as good as the Indians. Four hundred years. I've lived in a place for five at the most, and that was when I was little.

"Today we'll do La Llorona, the Weeping Woman," Mrs. Lovato continues. "Does anybody know who La Llorona is?"

Tony Jaramillo and Ray Baca scoot looks at each other but they hold their tongues because they're boys and knowing something the teacher wants you to know isn't cool. Mrs. Lovato sighs and looks at them. "Tony? Ray?"

Ray squirms. "She's a witch lady," he mumbles. *"Loca."*

"Loca how?"

Ray studies his fingernails as if they're the most interesting things on earth. I sigh. He shrugs. "You know. Just crazy."

"How crazy? Tony?"

Tony knows he's stuck but still acts as if he's too cool for this. "She killed her kids," he says, lolling back in his chair. "And now she walks around the arroyos at night, crying and wearing all black."

Killed her kids? Who was this woman?

"Have you ever heard her crying?" Mrs. Lovato asks, but that's got to be too much. The white kids would all laugh.

Tony squirms just like his buddy Ray, and Mrs. Lovato laughs herself. "Okay, ninos. When I was a little girl, I thought I heard her."

Ray and Tony's eyes widen.

"Oh yes. Visiting *mi tia y tio en Nuevo Mexico.* Taos. In the night. It was this awful howling. Made me so scared I ran and got in bed with my auntie." Tony and Ray are speechless.

Now that she has them hooked, Mrs. Lovato moves fast. She glances at the rest of the class and says, "Okay. So why did she kill her children? There are a lot of different ways to tell this story. Tony, what's the reason your tio has told you?"

Tony answers, "'Cause some conquistador said he'd marry her if she dumped the kids."

My heart's a drum being pounded. *Have to keep Mr. Badger.*

Mrs. Lovato turns from the boys. "Class," she says. "According to Tony, why is La Llorona so unhappy?"

"'Cause she killed her kids!" cries Mary Ellen Richards, who's got two baby brothers and carries a doll around with her everywhere.

"Was she wrong to do this?"

"Yes!" A chorus of voices, mostly girls.

"What if she were very poor and the man was her only way to have a lot of food everyday? Or what if she were rich but jealous of other girlfriends he might have? That's a version I've heard."

Mary Ellen doesn't care about versions. She's red as the inside of a watermelon, and out of her chair. "Why is it men have all the food?" she shouts. "Or can have girlfriends when women can't have boyfriends? Why is it? Why?"

The boys start to snicker. "'Cause girls are dips," smirks one of them, under his breath.

Oh brother. Mary Ellen leaps out of her seat like a panther and right onto him. "Stop it!" she screams. "Stop it!" Swatting his head and her arms going everywhere. The boy who opened his mouth is fighting her off the way you do a swarm of bees.

Mrs. Lovato's over there in two seconds, trying to restrain her. Mary Ellen wipes the back of her hand over her face and I remember some rumor about Mary Ellen's dad beating her mom up.

Mrs. Lovato looks like she's just seen a ghost. When the class is calm again and Mrs. Lovato back at her desk, she pats her hair back into place and readjusts her dress. She starts to hand out La Llorona worksheets to color and read, from a kids' book on New Mexico folklore. I flip through it, kind of eyeing Mary Ellen off to my right. The mimeograph doesn't have a lot about killing the kids, or Mr. Badger the conquistador. That's *my* version. Some woman who'd actually *hate* her daughter for being a girl, and not even see what her Mr. Badger is doing… I start fuming just like Mary Ellen.

Where's all the stories about girls who aren't so stupid in front of men? Where's Nancy Drew and Laura Ingalls Wilder and those girls? Girls who would never kill their kids for some man? I'd rather read about mountain lions. At least they protect their cubs. I don't care if the mimeograph says it's just a story to keep kids out of arroyos when it rains, so they don't get killed in a flash flood. It's *not* just about that. It's not about that at all, and I don't know which I hate worse—what it's really about or the fact that the damn worksheet doesn't want to look it square in the face.

Three a.m. Mrs. O is on her second cup of tea. I'm rooting around like a raccoon for the courage to ask if I played a part in killing Lars when she bolts toward the window.

"What is it?" I ask.

Mrs. Oodegaard tilts her head. "There's that light on again."

"Why are you whispering?"

She blushes slightly as if she hasn't noticed. "Sorry. But that light makes me feel as though they can see me."

"It comes on a lot?"

"About half the time, when I'm up too. I don't like it."

"Sarah lives there."

She swivels back to me. "So you *do* know Sarah!"

I take a step back. "Yes, of course. She visits me."

"Like this?" she asks, gesturing at my golden buckskin.

My turn to blush. "Er, ah, no. As a skeleton."

Mrs. Oodegaard keeps a smile from breaking out. "I see. I'm honored you would change yourself so for me."

"She…um…never knew about me differently. She found me. Up the hillside one day."

"She finds a lot of people." But Mrs. Oodegaard doesn't say anymore about this, and I go back to looking at the light.

"Why do you think the light is on?" I ask.

"I don't know. She says it's because her father can't sleep at night. But I could tell that was a lie. In fact, that's when she told me about you. Changed the subject right away and looked to the hillside and told me about you."

"Pretty big secret."

"Yes," she says.

There's a silence and I think I better get this over with. "Mrs. O?" I ask.

"Yes?"

"Did I kill Lars?"

"What?" She jerks away from the window like a horse seeing a snake. "What on earth makes you say that?"

So I tell her about the day I got to Lars with my stories about evolution, and how I found out later he was going to step off into a shaft because of what I had said. I look down at my feet. "So ever since—"

"Oh, Ouray," she says, and tries to touch my arm, but I am just air. "Let me read you something."

She disappears into the back and comes back with a worn out piece of paper in her hands. "I found this letter in his dresser after he died," she says. "I don't suppose you can read it yourself?"

I shake my head. I could, slowly, just the way I read those newspapers in the trash in front of Lars' shack. But the funny feeling about writing comes back—white folks have the weakest memories and have to rely on writing things down all the time. What good is that? Besides, I want to hear her read. I want to hear Lars through her.

"Well," she says, and shakes out the paper, "this ought to set your mind at ease." I look over her shoulder while she reads.

Dear Maddy,

I have never been shaken in my faith until we came out of Nebraska and into southwestern Colorado. As you know, I never held to my father's brand of it, and I never felt ashamed for not holding to it. I always felt much better in church with you and other Lutherans, come West from Minnesota or Norway or Sweden as we did. But the funeral for Jose Baca down in Ignacio was my first taste of something which shook me, and I believe it shook me only because it was a re-connection to something I have felt all my life but refused to admit was God. If you recall, you and I were early to that service. We were early because we wanted to see the Ute land and to eat lunch down there at the little cafe across from the church. But when we walked by the church you smelled lavender and had to peek in. Spanish women were scrubbing the church, floor to ceiling, in lavender water. Why? you asked them. Because, they said, it cleans. And then a man came up, a priest, and said when he was on mission in Africa they put lavender all over the floors, so that when people walked on them, the plant was crushed and scent was released. It kept away the mosquitoes, said the priest.

The church was of wood, bending with age and use, polished in places, worn in others, falling apart. It leaned. There were triptychs of biblical scenes, many with the Virgin Mary, made of wood and hinged and painted in a simple way. The cross was large and wooden and had an especially bloody Jesus on it. He wept blood, if I remember. The whole funeral, I could not keep my eyes off of him, nor my brain from smelling lavender at every breath, and instead of feeling sorrowful, dark thoughts for Jose, who lost his life too young in the mine, my body kept feeling the oddest elation. When we walked back outside, the far mountains (for they are far down in Ignacio) and the several clouds and the sun on the grass radiated the most amazing light. I wanted to paint then; I understood what it must be like to be Monet, or Van Gogh, or those other artists we saw on display once in Denver. I was not myself for several days.

Then Ouray happened. I don't know how to tell you about Ouray. To this day, I don't know how to do this. Dear Wife, I see a ghost. Dear Maddy, I talk to a ghost. What would you say to that? I did tell you a few times, that I swore I saw his countenance, but you just said, He has been dead forty years. You didn't make fun of me, thank God, but in a way your answer was even worse because it assumed such resignation toward my mental state. As if you had accepted, without question, my odd manias and slumps. You see, Maddy, I have never accepted them. I am in agony about them.

Ouray drove me mad once, when I was deep in a lament. He came into my bookkeeping shack in front of the main shaft and explained evolution to me in a way that made such utter sense I did not know what to do. I realized then that I have been in secret admiration of Mr. Darwin ever since I heard about him, and I heard about him first in theology school, where he was set upon as a godless mind full of the most corrupt notions. And then when I smelled the lavender, and noticed the light afterwards, I put it all together. Darwin wasn't doing anything but noticing *God!* And *God* was nothing more than the most brilliant passion pouring through every living creature! How could I have devoted myself to an entire Christian sect bent on denying this aspect of God? A taciturn sect, un-effusive, set on faith and faith only, in Jesus and Jesus only, to save our souls. But I didn't need Jesus to save my soul! I was saved the minute I walked into that smell of lavender; the second I grasped what it meant to *weep blood*; the blinding moment of walking back out into a world so full of beauty I hardly knew where to put it. I tell you, Maddy, it was the most intensely spiritual moment of my life, and it looked like nothing my Lutheran training, not to mention my father's more fundamentalist beliefs, ever prepared me for.

The dangers in denying this passion became readily apparent to me. Men might see themselves as good only if they worked too hard at something they loathed but that other people approved of, since a life of their own passion would be labeled selfish and dangerous. (Unless, of course, that passion matched perfectly with Christian duty, in which case there is no duty.) But otherwise these men would become clotted with rage and too willing to release it through spirits and gunfights. Or they might shrivel up into bitter old men, and die alone. Just look at my father. That's what happened to him.

To wait for the gifts of heaven when there is so much here on Earth!

And women. Women are denied their passion too. They are subjugated and corseted and told to keep their minds and bodies shut, for nothing in the human species resembles that potential for Godly life as much as a ripe woman. Yet ripe women, in our culture, are to be closeted (if they are "good") or scorned (if they are "bad"). Men rape women out of the same kind of rage which makes them drink too much and put fists through others' mouths. Men rape women the way they rape land. Always wanting what is denied in themselves, then destroying what it is they want when they get near it. Men slaughter animals without a second thought, having been given "dominion" over them to do as we will. Oh yes, we were supposed to be "stewards" but this assumes a responsibility we men (and I do mean men) as creatures have never earned. Don't you see, Maddy? You can't be put in charge of something unless you've worked for it! And few of our men, I daresay, have done so.

Ouray made me start to read. I read on all the faiths. Do you know that no other faith puts woman as lesser than man in the eyes of God? As an outgrowth of a mere "rib"? Do you know that no other faith, in its doctrine at least, blames her so readily for all the sins of the world? That no other faith assumes we can *name* the plants and animals? The audacity! Do you have any notion of how *self-centered* we are, we Christians who preach selflessness but scoff when Indians refer to the animals as their "brothers"? Who refer to sage brush as their "grand-mother"? Ouray did this all the time! And what did I do? I laughed at him.

Now, you tell me, Maddy. Who has the bigger heart? An Indian who can weep honestly to the sage, and include it on equal footing with himself, or a Christian man who cannot treat his own wife as an equal, much less the plants and animals? And what have we done to this country, Maddy, as a result? What have we done?

Mrs. O puts the letter down. How odd that all my taunting paid off with this! I can't believe anything good came out of it. I finger the letter, yellow and creased in her hands. I feel blown clean, wind coming through ponderosa.

My hands stay on the letter. Mrs. O hands it to me and I keep gazing at it.

"What are you thinking?" she asks, finally.

"I miss him," I say. At last another human who could have stood on Kit Carson's porch with me and seen the enormous gap between white and Indian. Who might have seen the gap in me. Who could have talked to me, stitching the two halves of myself back together.

I clutch the letter, sinking slowly to the floor, cross-legged. "I miss him," I say again, to the bottom of her dresser. The letter sits, almost glowing, in my lap, while my other hand cups my forehead. "Ohhh," I say, as the bittersweet aftertaste of missed possibility wells up all around me, Lars a best friend I never got to have.

Later, back in my crevice, I am contrite. When I see Mrs. O again, I say, "You know, we Utes weren't perfect, either. Lars made it seem so."

"No," she says. "Being human, I imagine you were not. But do you see now? You didn't kill him. You made him think. Isn't that what you wanted to do?"

I'm quiet. Maybe. Maybe not. Maybe I hadn't wanted to do anything but terrify somebody because I was mad at all that had happened to my people. A part of me is still happy I made him think, but mostly I'm more upset with myself than ever.

"We laughed at our women too, sometimes," I say, still grasping at imperfections, trying to make her see. "We laughed at them when we were young and full of ourselves. Rape happened. Most things with women were about being young and insecure, though."

"But then you grew up, I take it."

"Most times."

"How did that happen?"

I tip my head toward the mountains. "Initiations. Learning to hunt, fight. Lot of boys died doing that. Also sweats, vision quests. You have no food for three days and only a thin blanket, you face things."

"Did women do these quests?"

I shook my head. "No need for them to. Their bodies did it for them in a way. No shame in that; we had ceremonies for them when they started to bleed with the moon. That part was private. When they came back, though—aaiiee, the whole tribe had a party." I smile at that. Bear dances, meeting a girl behind the pinon trees on a night with no moon, playing flute for her outside the tipi like some horny coyote. But then I shake my head. "I think boys need something more. There's nothing *in* them, the way there is in women. No babies to carry for nine moons, no childbirth to get through, no instant hungry mouth to get food for. We have to be shaped in a different way."

"So Lars was right. You have to earn it."

I nod. "Yes. Or you stay a baby forever, and a baby in a man's skin destroys most of what he touches."

Next night, the light's on again. "That day of the fire," I say.

"What about it?"

"That's when I saw you, finally. But before that, I saw her brother light it."

Mrs. Oodegaard shakes her head. "Angry boy, that Ricky."

"If it'd been my son, I'd have sent him off on a bad horse with no food for a few days."

She brightens. "You had a son?"

"Yes."

"Well, there you go. I had two."

"I know."

She turns back to the window. "One of them lives up near Meeker." She shoots an arrow from her eyes at me. "Sorry. Bad place for you, I know. Anyhow, he's got his dad's disease, though they have medication for that now. My other son lives near Denver."

I don't know what to say, and I don't know if I can talk about my own son. I go back to looking at the light from across the yard. "Do you think those kids are safe?" I ask.

She glances sharply at me, an owl in search of food. "Do you?"

I see Sarah caving in around her crotch after her brother pushed her down. The tea party she made for herself wearing that flower dress in February comes back, that time when I wondered why she was all alone and where her mother was. The home in the house of oak, all by herself.

"No," I say.

She waits for me to say why, but all I have is my mouth, straight as a snake in the sun.

She gets the drift. "Well, then," she says, standing up, dumping the rest of her tea down the drain. "Let's go see."

"What?"

"Let's go see," she repeats, and gestures toward the window, the light faintly streaming and reaching out toward us, along that endless stretch of grass.

Earthsong

There seems to be no way for either one of them to talk about what they see. In fact, their heads float straight to the clouds shrouding our highest points, our tallest spikes of granite, and with them come the snow geese cackling after them, cackling for them to Say it, Say it, please Say it, because we can't say it, not we geese who mate for life and wear white and only know the hardship of long migrations and scarce food.

But Ouray and Madeleine Oodegaard are even more silent than the geese have been on this subject, whatever it is. They're shaking, really, though Ouray seems to be boiling toward some breaking point and we're afraid he'll explode into a million fragments all over our rocks. Mrs. Oodegaard lays a steady hand on him precisely as she used to lay a steady hand on her skittish husband—we saw that once when they climbed up here with their boys—and it has the same effect.

A little calmer, he walks over to a precipice and asks the Great Spirit why white people were ever invented, why they had to come here, why they would do that to their children when didn't they know how precious it was to have a child at all and Oh Great Spirit my Paron, my Paron…

Paron? Mrs. Oodegaard asks. And he says, My son. My son. They took him, the Lakota did, and the Arapaho raised him, and once, long time later, they promised me if I signed a treaty I could have him back. He was a young man by then, though, and claimed he did not know me. Claimed he wasn't even Ute, though they called him Ute Friday and everybody seemed to know where he'd come from.

But he didn't know me! Looked me straight up and with eyes just like mine and said he didn't know me. I ripped open his shirt and found the scar where the horse had run him through a limb when he was five. Tell me you are not Paron, I said.

But my enemies had taught him well. He glared in his Arapaho buckskin and said, I do not know you.

Ouray starts to howl, and crumples on our flank, sobbing into his hands the way men do when they'd rather have no one see. If he were alone, we suspect he'd scream at the top of his lungs into our echoing cliffs, or maybe cut his hair or his forearms the way grieving two-leggeds used to do in the past.

The birds do a magnificent thing then. They come to him, and nestle on his shoulders. Soft feathers touch his brow. They start to coo, and one of them looks back to us, and says, This is what we do for the children.

Mrs. Oodegaard stares as mute witness. But her head, more sensible at this moment than Ouray's, is already leaving us. Already she's halfway down on the ground, and recognizing we have a conduit, we follow her. A few geese waddle after us, babbling No, no, it'll be too hard; but we answer, scoffing, What can be worse than being scorched from a volcano? Being formed from the belly of fire?

You'll see, they say, You will see. Telling you is one thing, seeing it another!

They're frantic. But we brush them off and follow the spirit of Mrs. Oodegaard. Down below, she's tugging at Ouray's sleeve, away from something she desperately wants to leave.

We peer in the window. What we see sends the sensation of our insides being scorched right back to us again, just as they were all those millions of years ago. In a flash, the flash of his camera on her little girl flanks, the volcanoes roar up in us, a molten horror flooding our capacity for speech. We know this! We choke out to the geese. We know this! As the geese, the good, white geese, in their feathery love, beat on the pane and Mrs. Oodegaard lets go of Ouray to beat on the pane also.

Yes! Good for you, old woman! Beat more, beat louder, anything against that fire inside!

At the sound he looks up in terror, and snaps off the light.

Inky darkness. Harder and harder for us to see. We lose Mrs. Oodegaard, who seems to have gone too deep into shock or sorrow or anger for us to reach her anymore, and we hear only his footsteps fleeing up the stairs. Mrs. Oodegaard beats the pane again, for Sarah, but this has the same effect as on her father. There is a slight noise in the dark, and then her softer footsteps, following him.

Part Three

Snares

BARBARA

The phone is ringing at four a.m. Ringing and ringing. I roll toward it from the murky undertow of sleep. "Christ," mutters Trent Sr., and puts a pillow over his head.

"'Lo?" I answer, thick-tongued.

"Barbara? Barbara, this is Madeleine Oodegaard. I have—I have to talk to you. I don't know what to do!"

I sit up on an elbow. "What on earth is wrong? Are you all right?" God, maybe she's having a heart attack. But Maddy's sensible enough; she'd call 911 for that, wouldn't she?

"I'm fine," says Maddy. "But that little Graves girl—Sarah Graves next door, my little neighbor girl, Trent's friend—"

"Sarah? Yes? What about Sarah?" My stomach curdles a little. "What about her?"

"Oh Lord, Barbara, I've never seen anything like it. In all my days…" Maddy makes a kind of half-sob, half-choke, as if she just ate a bad piece of meat and wants to regurgitate it.

"Seen what? What are you talking about?"

Maddy starts keening. "Oh Lord, Barbara. I'm so sorry."

"What do you mean?"

He's—he's *exploiting* her, Barbara."

"What do you mean?" Stuck record, I sound like a stuck record.

"Sexually. Her father is sexually exploiting her."

"Oh my God." I sit back on the bed. I can feel flames lapping inside of me, or dry ice, the cold-hot feeling of shock.

"Barbara? Barbara?"

"I'm here." But I still can't talk for a minute. Maddy doesn't say anything this time either, until I can ask, "How did you find out about this?"

"Well, I—ah—I've seen a light on there at night a great deal. You see, lately I can't sleep much in the middle of the night, something about Lars, I suppose, still after me. But after watching her and talking to you, and what with that light coming on—well, I did an unneighborly thing. I walked over there in the dark and peered in the window. And oh, Lord—"

"What, Maddy? What exactly did you see?"

"Pornography," she whispers. "I saw him using her for—pornography."

OURAY

That sonofabitch I will kill his hide. I will string him out on all four limbs, a horse on each limb, and tear him to pieces.

I go back to my crevice but I'm too big for it now. I thrash at oak in the dark and rip out grass like a deer gone mad.

That sonofabitch. I will personally see that he suffers no end, no end, no end…

BARBARA

"Trent Sr., wake up."

My husband wipes his eyes and sits up. "What is it? Who was that?"

"Maddy Oodegaard. You know, my old Sunday School teacher whose husband…"

"Oh, yeah." Trent Sr. takes a drink of water from the glass next to his side of the bed. "What'd she want?"

"She lives next door to Sarah, and…well…" I look down at my hands. "Trent, I have to tell you something and it won't be very pleasant."

So I do. When I'm through, we stare at each other in the dusk of our room.

Trent Sr. brings an arm around my head, bending me toward him. "Gotta call the cops, sweetie," he says.

"But what evidence do we have, other than Maddy's own eyes and all this behavior on Sarah's part that suddenly makes sense to me now?"

"None. But Sarah's gotta get out of there, right?"

"Ye-es."

"So we can't take her legally until the law's involved."

"Take her…?" I stare at him.

"Why, sure. Who else, honey? Who else do you want Sarah to go to? She sure as hell can't stay in that house."

I don't know whether to laugh or to cry. Another child! Maybe two, what with her brother, too. And for how long? Good God.

I start to tell him he's crazy, but stop halfway through. He often sees three moves ahead of me, a skill honed from furniture-making. I'm used to that. And I'm used to the fact that he doesn't say much a lot of the time. But the surprise—even after years of marriage—is that when he does say something, there's a clean intelligence to it. Like a work horse who suddenly reveals a compassionate smartness beyond everything his plodding bigness would imply.

OURAY

"Ouray? Ouray? Where are you?"

I can hear her calling for me on the cold air the river brings, but I'm halfway up the valley already, going back to Philistine. I haven't been there in so many seasons but he's going to go there, Luke Graves is going to go there when he's found out. I know it, I can feel it, and if he heads off somewhere else I'll drag him back here. I'm going to make him sweat the biggest sweat of his life. Until he vomits or burns. Until all that evil drips out of him and scorches the ground beneath his feet.

"Ouray?"

Mrs. O is weeping a little now, and I almost turn around. But the telephone she explained to me—how you could talk to someone over the wires I've seen strung along the road—rings. I can see light in the east, pushing back the darkness, and hear her voice sniffing. Something about police, going to the police in the morning. Yes, yes, she says. We'll go. I can't hear the other end of the conversation, but talking seems to calm her down.

She stops weeping, hangs up, doesn't call for me anymore. Goes to clean herself, get ready for the day. I pick up my rocks, and twelve cut stalks of willow, and float on. Toward Philistine. Toward the scene of crimes committed by white men with too much greed in their hearts and one Indian too mad about it to see clearly. I picked a harmless clairvoyant instead, one with, it turns out, the same vision of God I had.

Damn me. Damn him.

Who is this sweat going to be for anyway?

MADDY

The La Plata County Sheriff's Department roosts in an old brick building on Main, next to the Post Office. The two buildings might have been twins, as if some architect could only conceive of giving birth to a couplet. Or so I think. Barbara and I wait without a word for our turn with the sergeant. I clutch my white vinyl purse and Barbara sucks on a thumbnail. *What are we doing here?* Will they believe a couple of women with suicidal husbands and burned sons to their names? *And why do I persist in that ridiculous feminine belief that I am a lesser being by virtue of my contact with the wounds of others?*

Stop. I take a Kleenex out of my purse and wipe my glasses. I issue a little prayer to the Lord because I know I'm in what I call one of my Point-Counterpoint moods. Think one thought, come back with a contrary one. Two halves of my brain, fighting. It always happens when I feel unsure of myself, and if I do it long enough, I'll drive myself crazy. This kind of thinking, if I can even call it that, went on for months after Lars died.

"Mrs. Oodegaard?"

We both look up, and I start smiling in spite of everything. "Why, Roger Matthieson. Haven't seen you in years!" I wink at Barbara. "Another Sunday School student. The generation after you. Like you, he has not returned to the fold."

Roger's neck shades to a rough pink over his stubbly beard. Relief fans through me. He can't think we're completely absurd if he knows me in some other way than what the county coroner had to say five years ago.

"Let's go in my office," he says, "and you can tell me the problem."

We follow him down the hall, to a door marked "Investigations." Sergeant Matthieson opens it for us, and we go on through. Two blue office chairs are offered to us, modern and plastic.

He listens to my story. I start on edge but gain strength quickly, faltering only over my own guilt at playing spy on my neighbors and trying to keep Ouray out of it. I find it hard. I want to include him the way you include old friends in whatever adventure happens to be going on at the moment. I want to give him credit.

But I hold my tongue and Sergeant Matthieson turns to Barbara. When we're through, he blinks at us. He reminds me of a sweet roan draft horse I had when I was a teenager. That horse was the nicest thing you ever saw, and he worked harder than any other we had. After a minute the sergeant leans back in his chair and says, "Pretty serious stuff, Mrs. Oodegaard."

He says my name like "Miz Oodegaard." As if some Southern strain hadn't been knocked out of his speech in spite of growing up around here. I gaze at him, silent. Expressionless, but with a mighty will leaking out of me that I've worked at a long time. It has made countless good Lutherans out of the children of St. Paul's, that gaze. I held my own children to their rights with it, too.

Roger sees my gaze and stands up. "Kind of makes you sick, doesn't it?"

He looks out the window, then back at us. "Okay," he says. "Here's what we do. We get us a search warrant. If he's taking pictures the way you say he is, he ought to have them hidden somewhere."

"You can get a search warrant just like that?" Barbara asks, and I know she feels as if we're trying to push for a trial with no solid evidence.

"All it takes is probable cause, Miz MacIntosh. Probable cause from a credible witness. And I have that. But I'll also go ahead and have you, Miz MacIntosh, talk to our Child Protective Services counselor. Who'll write down the behaviors you've witnessed and come up with a report that'll state the likelihood of that behavior coming from an abused child. But I don't need to do that for the warrant."

"That's all it takes?" I ask. "Me peeking in the window and seeing—"

Roger nods. "Sure. If you're a credible witness. Which you are."

"I am? I'm just an old woman, and I was married to a...a..."

Roger cuts me off. I see ruddy knuckles descend to his desktop and he makes me look him straight in the eye. "Miz Oodegaard, in case you haven't figured it out, most of this town admires the hell out of your fortitude and sanity in the face of all of that. Now, I will see you back here this afternoon at three p.m."

My mouth is working in the way I know old women's mouths do when they're not used to being one-upped like that. Barbara takes my hand. "Come on, you old mule," she mutters, smiling. "I know it's against your religion, but learn how to take a compliment when it comes."

SARAH

I'm playing with my paho, home from school, when there's a knock on the door. Ricky's out on the back patio with his Joe Businessman money, and Mom's shut away in her office, so I answer it.

Two policemen stand there, and a woman with a long braid.

"Sarah Graves?" one of them, a tall guy with red hair, asks.

"That's me."

"Sergeant Matthieson," he says, and puts his hand out for me to shake. I take it, but I don't know what's going on. He turns to the man next to him and says, "This is my partner, Lieutenant Rico." Lieutenant Rico also sticks out his hand. They seem incredibly polite.

"And I'm Carole Pike," the Braid Lady says.

I look at her. "Are you a policeman too?"

She laughs. "No. I'm a social worker."

"Is your mom home?" Sergeant Matthieson asks.

"Yeah. I can go get her." I turn on my heels and go down the hall. "Mo-o-m! There's some policemen here."

I hope something bad hasn't happened to Dad up at the college. Blew up a test tube in geochemistry or something. Why else would they be here? My stomach balls up like a pillbug, but then Mom's at the door, and I forget everything else.

It's like Mom is an electric power station, or clothes static-y from the dryer, or a nebula like the ones Dad has postcards of. I stand back, still as a mouse. Nobody'll tell me to leave if I can stay invisible. I kind of sink into the kitchen cabinets, Mom's back to me across the room and the policemen's view of me blocked by her.

"Miz Graves, we...ah...have a warrant to search your house," Sergeant Matthieson says, and pulls something out of his front pocket.

"You do? What for?" Mom seems puzzled at first and then a little huffiness creeps in.

Carole Pike puts a light hand on Mom's shoulder. "Mrs. Graves, why don't you have a seat?"

Ooh boy. Not the tone to take with Mom.

"Don't patronize me," she snaps, sure enough, batting away Miss Pike's hand. "I have a Ph.D. from Princeton, thank you very much. Now just what is going on?"

Carole and the policemen nod a tiny bit at each other and the policemen slip off downstairs. My eyes bug out. The basement. *The basement!*

But Mom is flailing her arms and shouting. "What is going on?"

"So you don't know of your husband's activities, then?"

Husband's activities. But Mom turns three shades of red then and I can feel a knife go into my gut. *Hurt my mom. Never hurt anyone. Selfish people hurt*— I hold my breath. What to do? Go to Mom? Stay silent? Mom! Dad! What—? Where—? I'm so confused I don't do anything.

"Of course! Of course not!" Mom's saying. "What activities?" Her eyes jag like crazy around the room, looking for a way out. She reminds me of a fish that's just been caught and wants back in the water more than anything in the world.

Carole Pike's mouth goes stiff. "Your husband—"

"Bingo!" comes a cry from the basement.

"Bingo, what? What have they found?" Mom's really crazy now, has that look when she's about to faint.

"They found pictures, I believe, Mrs. Graves. Pictures of your daughter being used for child pornogra—"

I can't hold it anymore. *Ceiling, ceiling* gargoyle pose, crouched on the light fixture. Can't breathe. Mom clutches the table, then jerks as if she wants to slap Carole. But then she seems to think no, better not, and instead lifts herself out her chair enough to grab the phone on the wall behind Carole's head. She dials fast.

"What're you doing?" Carole asks, pulling on the cord. "Roger! Mike! Get up here!"

A file drawer slams and I can hear heels on the wooden stairs. But Mom already has Dad on the line. "Luke! Luke! They're—"

Can't stand the hysterics in her voice. *Luke! Luke!* Like she'll lose it any minute the way she used to in church or in the shopping center and Ricky and I wanted to be ten million miles away.

"Mrs. Graves, PUT THAT PHONE DOWN."

Mom cups her hand over the receiver, back to not being hysterical except that I can see the phone shake. "I have a right to call my husband, don't I?"

Sergeant Matthieson is really trying to restrain himself. "He's a criminal, now, Mrs. Graves. You are aiding and abetting a criminal."

"Luke? Luke, did you hear that? I can't believe what they're say—" But Matthieson's lost it and is waving a picture in her face, while the other one jerks the phone out of her hands.

Mom seems to see the picture and let go of the phone all at once. My ears are full of sand and the world's spinning; my ears are an hourglass someone just tilted totally upside down. Mom kind of shrieks and melts onto the dining room table.

I fall out of the gargoyle pose from the ceiling. I can't stop this awful spinning. "Nooo, nooo! Don't hurt my mom!" I stumble to her, trying to hug her. "I didn't mean to hurt you, Mom!"

But Mom looks at me like I'm some monster. She backs off of me like if she touched me she'd be burned by acid. "You!" she shrieks. "You!" And I know I've hurt her, I know it's all my fault, I know—La Llorona—I want to run; I need to run; my life—my life—but she's got me and she's pushing at me around the corner to the basement stairs and she weeps and yells and screams at me. I think I hear the word "whore" and maybe something about *How could you* but the ocean's back in my ears and Miss Pike's struggling with her from behind and then Mom pushes again right at the top of the steps, with my heels off in the air and my arms trying to grab anything.

My mommy pushes me My mommy pushes me My mommy pushes me My mommy... Sergeant Matthieson's got me in his hairy red arms but it doesn't even matter. It doesn't even matter because what I thought all along is true. *My mother will kill me My mommy tried to kill me My mommy...* all of those basement steps and I will dream about sailing down them, I will dream about the blackness, I will I will I will the world will go dark and I will die, over and over and over again.

Sweat

I can't move for heartbeats. I've got everything ready up at Philistine, and now I'm hovering outside the Graves' house with my ears ringing because Sinewav the Creator just took a giant handaxe and beat the rock faces of the peaks with it. Everything rings, the world's suddenly huge and empty and I can't even remember what one strand of dewy grass looks like in the morning sun. I saw Sarah's mother using that telephone, and I heard the name Luke, and I was thinking, Where is he? because that's who I'd come for, when she pushed Sarah, pushing and pushing, and tried to fling her down the stairs. Tried to kill her own daughter.

My throat's gone as parched as corn. I can't breathe; I make moves toward the house but I see the big man with red hair's got her, and the other one, brown as tobacco, has the mother, and there's a woman with braids who has just almost slapped the mother's face and then retracts her paw as if she can't believe she stepped out of herself like that. So even though now all I want to do is kill that mother, and I don't know which is worse, the mother or the father, I start breathing again and feel the grass come back and the quiet little pinons telling me what I can do. I put a feather on Sarah's doorstep—an eagle feather, the best one I still have—and slink over to Mrs. Oodegaard's.

"Mrs. O!" I call. "Mrs. O!"

"Here, Ouray." She's at the kitchen window, straining to see anything over there. The front of the Graves' house is on the other side from her house, though, so she can't see much.

"What's happening?"

"Mrs. Oodegaard, Great Spirit, I just saw—" But I stop. Too complicated, too long, she'll hear it later. "Where is Luke Graves?" I say.

"Luke?" She looks at me blankly. "How should I know?"

"Where does he go during the day? Every day he leaves and goes somewhere in that Iron Horse car with no tracks and no other cars next to it. Like the red fire ones, only smaller. Where does he go?"

"Oh! You mean where does he *work*," she says, as if the sun suddenly came out from behind a cloud in her brain. "At the college. Up on the mesa above town." She points in the general direction.

I slouch. "There's a lot of buildings up there."

"He's a geologist. Look for signs for geology." She spells it out for me on a piece of paper. "It'll look like that."

"Thank you," I say.

"Wait!" she calls to me, as I fly out the door. "What are you going to do?"

"You'll see!" And I'm off, up to the mesa with the college.

I don't even have to go find the geology building. I see his Iron Horse thing in a flat area with a bunch of others like it. But I know his; it's blue and bigger than most of the others. And then I see him running toward it. *Sonofabitch*. I can't believe that wife of his.

He gets in the Iron Horse thing, his car, and actually does start going up the road toward Philistine. He drives very fast and I have to hold on in the way back so I don't get sick. We lurch around sharp corners and he works the Horse hard up hills. Past the place where people with planks on their feet ride chairs up the mountain and then slide back down on the planks ("Skiing," said Kit Carson. "It's called skiing," but I never did get the point of it). He pulls off—to an old two-track that people used when they were cutting the forest around here long time ago. He drives the Horse right into a thicket of willow after banging along for a good while on this road. I think he's trying to hide the Horse as well as he can.

I gauge where we are. Philistine is still north of here, but not by that much. Luke goes around back and opens up the rear of the

Horse behind me. I jump, and ooze outside. He finds a little pack for his back, some water, a sweater, boots. Geology gear, I guess. Sarah says geologists study rocks, so Luke must spend a lot of time outside.

The two-track turns into a deer trail. Luke looks around, deciding whether to take that or bushwhack it somewhere else. The earth's working in my favor—it's steep up above him and steep down below, and full of brush and fir trees. He squats down at the dirt of the deer trail, swipes his hand on it. Dry.

I give him one. He's not stupid. He's checking to see if he'd leave tracks.

Luke starts up the trail. He doesn't look evil. If anything he looks bland, like the inside of a potato. Easygoing, with brown hair going thin on top, and blue eyes. He's in good shape—not fat, not too thin, and maybe even handsome, though what whites consider good looking makes no sense to me.

The sun goes low over the peaks to the west, so it starts to cool and darken. Across the canyon the light still shines on all the new leaves of aspen just beginning to bud out. He keeps walking awhile. I follow, just making sure that if he veers off this path toward somewhere else other than Philistine, I can tackle him and move him back on.

But he seems to know where he's going. There's a purpose in his walk. Not much hesitation. Maybe he knows the mine.

It's deep twilight by the time we come to it. Lars' bookkeeping shack is now a fan of two-by-fours, rotting on the ground. Grass grows where the tents used to be. The chute still stands, but the spur tracks were ripped up long ago. When I first came up here with the equipment for the sweat, I was glad to see how much it had started to disappear back into the ground.

Luke finds a boulder and sits down in front of Lars' shack. The old main shaft of the mine yawns off to his right, and he pulls out some nuts and a little water. He looks at the boulder he's sitting on quizzically, as if to say, What's that doing here? and then pulls a bottle from his pack. He unscrews the lid, extracting a dropper with fluid in it. Three drops of liquid hit the yellow rock next to his rear end. I stare. Bubbles form, and I can hear the slight hiss of rock dissolving. Three more drops, another frothing of stone. Like horses' mouths after they've been run too hard.

Luke Graves sits back and rocks. His eyes close momentarily, as if he is straining to listen to a music no one else can hear. When they open, suddenly, he stands upright and turns toward me.

I almost choke. Luke's blue eyes are deeper than any lake I've ever seen, clear and icy. They see right through me, but they get me, too. Like walking into a wasp's nest and not being able to see what's stinging you.

Luke smiles at nothing. The bottle with the dropper lies at his feet. He picks it up to put back in his pack, but not before squeezing the dropper one last time.

"Plink, plink, plink," he says, as he pours a final three drops on the rock.

Bubbles, the low hiss.

"Limestone," he mutters. And pivots away up the hill.

I flash ahead of him, and materialize in his path. We're exactly where Lars laughed at me for being an Indian who'd been to a zoo. There's a little clearing there, and behind me I've got the sweat poles and rocks in a pile. I dangle my fringe and he freezes.

Twilight, the trees so quiet it's like prayer time in the morning before the world awakens, air going cold on my skin. Luke still hasn't moved. But then he licks his lips, and I think his eyes have filled up with fear. The fear is so much better than that hideous emptiness I just saw by the hissing rock. I make my move.

"Ouray," I say, extending a hand in an ironic parody of that ridiculous way whites greet each other. I wouldn't want to take his hand to save my life.

He still just gapes at me.

"Come now, a man of science such as yourself? Surely you can assimilate me somehow." I can't stop grinning. I love the big words. This is better than Lars by a hundred elk hides.

"Ouray," I say again. "I am Chief Ouray."

"The—ah—Ute Chief?" He manages to speak. His voice is dry as sticks.

"That's right," I say.

"But—you're *dead.*" Again, that hoarse attempt at language.

"Depends on your definition of dead, I guess."

His eyes pop wider then, his mouth dangling like a baby's in sleep. Then he sags, slowly almost, into a heap. I move over toward him, glowing like a giant firefly. "Leave me alone," he mutters, arms covering his face. I sniff. Piss. Smells like piss.

I grab his pants. Wet. Great Spirit.

"Get up," I spit, jerking him to his feet by his collar. I'm so disgusted I want to kill him. Raping little girls and then peeing your pants first time you see a ghost. Great Spirit.

Luke rots beside me. I hiss at him. I hiss, "You and I got some work to do."

MADDY

It's almost night now, and I can't see the elk down in the floodplain anymore. I finish my soup and head for the linen closet to make my bed. But I find that my linen closet is a mess. Sheets spill out of it, a few blankets. Putting them back, I note that a few items are missing. A pair of sheets, the old white ones, thank goodness, not my best florals. And three—no, four—blankets. But who took them? And why?

Darn ghost. It must be Ouray. No one else has been anywhere near this house. I didn't know ghosts could steal. I put my fingers to my lips, thinking about him, about his asking where Luke works.

I take out the florals, go make my bed. I get in and turn out the light. Hmmphf. Well, I hope whatever he's doing, he puts them to good use.

"Draw a circle about four feet in diameter," I tell him, handing him a stick with a sharp point on the end and pointing toward the clearing. I've swept it free of pine duff and cones.

Luke does as he's told. He's still shaking and his pants stink. His eyes are dulled, the fear banking back there somewhere, a fire he's trying to keep in control, and with a weak hand he takes the stick and draws the circle in the dust.

"Good. Now, take the mallet while I hold the pole." I hand him a heavy mallet as I hold a steel stake on the ground along a point of the circle. I nod for Luke to pound until the stake has gone in four or five inches. "Good, considering you're shaking." I pull the stake up, and then go around the circle, making eight evenly spaced holes. Luke is sweating by the time we are done, even if it's night by now and the air is cold. The exercise seems to have stopped his fear, though, and he finds the energy to glare at me for the first time.

"What are we doing? I could just walk away, you know."

I shrug. "Go ahead."

We gaze at each other. Luke's chest swells up and down, breathing hard from swinging the mallet. Then he drops his eyes, his knees twitch, and he bolts.

"Godddamn sonofabitch—" I leap after him. Collar-grab again; you'd think these whites would learn what a disadvantage they are. I've killed more than one by virtue of his collar alone.

"Don't you know better than to run from a ghost?" Clenching that pathetic piece of cloth more tightly in my fist.

I breathe into his face. His hair ruffles up in response, but he's twisting his neck away from me. I want to let go of him. He stinks. Piss. Rage sweat. Rage sweat and piss, everywhere.

"Fine," he gags. "Just fine."

"You going to behave?"

He nods. I release him, but watch closely. He's back to shaking again. Good.

I prod him back to the clearing. "What next?" he mumbles.

I throw him a slick smile, the kind certain generals would throw us during treaty negotiations. I produce a pouch of tobacco and hand Luke a small canteen. "Pour a little water in each hole after I put some tobacco in."

"What for?"

"The medicine won't work otherwise."

Luke throws me a mean look out from under his fear, the look of the scientist who doesn't believe in hocus-pocus. They were always telling us what hooey our beliefs were, those scientists.

I stand up from putting tobacco in a hole. "Just do it," I sigh.

When we are done with that, I turn to the fresh cut stalks leaning up against a tree at the edge of the clearing. "Willow poles," I say. "Take one."

Luke does so. I take another. I teach him to put the fat end of the branch into one of the holes while I walk around to the opposite side. "Bend it in now, toward the middle. Be gentle. I cut these this afternoon so they should be okay, but you never know. I don't want them to crack."

The two ends overlap in the center of the circle. I take a strip of torn bedsheet (Mrs. Oodegaard won't mind, I'm sure) from my mouth and wrap the two together, tying them off. Then I press down on the bent, tied branches. "Hmm. Might have to lower the whole thing. But we can do that later."

"Lower?" Luke asks. "It's only four feet tall as it is."

"Be quiet," I say. "You have no idea what we're up to."

"It's a sweatlodge. I can see that."

I stand up in mild surprise from the willow pile, where I've gone to retrieve the next pair of poles. "Very good, Graves. Very good. Now shut up and let's do the next pair."

It takes us two hours to complete the grid of bent willow poles. When we're finished we have the skeleton of a lodge, a frame forming the round, low hut. By now it is totally dark, with stars glimmering above the trees, and no moon. Luke sits down all of a sudden.

"Whatsamatter?"

"Hungry," Luke says.

I fling him a sack of dried berries and beef jerky. He looks up with the surprised gratitude of a starving child.

"Just remember," I say. "All your life you've been far hungrier than you are now."

SARAH

After me and Ricky and Trent and Brandon go to bed, I take out the heart-shaped rock I got in Canyonlands once, the one I tried to give to Dad—only he left it on the picnic table at our campsite. Canyonlands is where he always wants to be. I bet he's there now.

I take out the heart-shaped rock and hold it under the covers with me. MacIntosh covers. Ricky's across the room from me. I stuffed the rock into my backpack along with my notebook and Miss Mouse and the paho and pictures of Mesa Verde when we were leaving our house for here. Right outside the door I found an eagle feather too. I couldn't believe it. I stuck it on my paho, so now it really looks like the ones in the books.

Mrs. MacIntosh went with us to get our stuff. She looked kind of green and furious at the same time, waiting outside for us while Miss Pike helped us. Mr. MacIntosh smiled at us when we walked into their house but later on I heard him say to Mrs. MacIntosh that he'd just as soon kill them both.

I wrap the rock tight in my hands. Ricky can't see. No one can see. I clutch it till my palms start sweating. I hold it, and then I take it— oh, what to do with it? Oh this is wrong, Oh, but, but *Daddy come back*, and I take it and hold it and then I put it between my legs.

Hours later, I call to Luke. "It's time," I say.

Luke wakes up from some kind of fanciful doze. I'd been watching him. Thinking how he changed all the time when we were putting up the lodge. Afraid one minute, angry the next, sly the next. Weasel. He glances at the bonfire, now reduced, that has been burning all night. "The rocks are hot?" he asks.

I nod. "When you go inside, go left till you sit opposite the door. If you get too hot, put your face down toward the floor along the outside ring. Or you can hold this up to your nose." I toss him a little bundle.

Luke sniffs. "Sage," he says, curious.

"Yup. Sage. The scent helps with the heat."

"How hot is it going to be?"

I can hear the fear back up his voice. Great Spirit, these evil types are such cowards. "What's that Spanish word?" I ask, more to myself than him. "*Macho*, that's it. This isn't a *macho* thing. The idea is not to see how much you can stand. The heat is just a way to bring out what needs to be brought out. It's a purification ceremony. The heat will not be the thing that makes your skin crawl. Not with you."

Luke throws me a sharp look. "I'm not an evil man," he says, the voice like sticks again. No moisture behind those words, no juice.

"Uh-huh," I say.

I hold the flap up, and Luke enters.

I start with seven rocks, black and full of small holes. They're dense and heavy and hold a huge amount of heat. "Vesicular basalt," I hear Luke murmur. I crawl inside after I've got all seven in the firepit in the middle and close the flap behind me.

The darkness is complete except for the glow of the rocks. Already it's quite warm. I sprinkle cedar on the rocks and the aroma of it fills the lodge.

"First round you pray for yourself. Can't pray for others till you learn to pray for yourself." I splatter water on the rocks and hot steam hisses into the dark.

"Prayer. Hmmphf."

"Don't believe in prayer?"

"To some God on high in a universe that hasn't existed since Copernicus blew the Pope's notion of how things work out of the water?"

I have no idea what he's talking about, but I can tell it's all head talk. I roll my eyes. "Be quiet. Sweat."

Luke begins to perspire. It is not the slow perspiration he would get on strenuous hikes in the mountains, either. It is an immediate downpour, a shower from the inside out. It reeks of rage. Utes always invited their enemies in for a sweat, because different emotions produce different sweats and then you can read their state of mind like deer tracks after rain. Luke, he's a cougar who has been shot and run up a tree. Rage and fear, the rage covering up the fear. *Never let them see you afraid.* Warrior talk. I cave in a little. That's what I did wrong with Paron. With that Lakota brave. He could see right into me, into that fear. I whiff my own armpits, and despair. It's not just Luke; rage courses in me, too.

A while later, Luke's breathing short little breaths that tell me he can't inhale too quickly because then the heat'll sting his nostrils.

"Breathe into your stomach. Deep. Slow."

"What?"

"You won't get dizzy that way." *And* you'll come face to face with whatever wolverine is clawing around in your gut.

He tries it out but I can tell this makes him intensely uncomfortable. He hasn't breathed into his stomach since childhood, probably, something he doesn't know until he's forced to try it.

Luke hurls another knife from his eyes at me. I'm drumming and singing across the fire. The drum pounds into Luke's heart, my heart, into the ground we're sitting on. Luke erases the lakes of sweat that form on his face every few minutes and tries to breathe regularly into his stomach and can't. He lets out an exasperated semi-gasp.

"Praying for yourself yet?" I ask, not breaking with the drumming.

Luke snorts and says nothing. He puts his face down to the floor as I suggested, and his body relaxes into the cooler air. He lies there, prone, sucking at air along the seam between dirt and the blanket covering the willow lodge. The rest of his body still sweats profusely.

"I always wanted to be an Indian," he says, down into the floor.

This surprises me. Chief Logic-man, an Indian? I had a scientist try to explain "logic" to me once. I began to tell him the mouse and fir tree story. He interrupted and told me that was "primitive animism" and that there was no logic to it. I left him up on a high meadow with a storm coming in. See if his logic could get him down.

"Indians think a great deal of the natural world," Luke says. "And I'm all for wilderness preservation."

"The 'natural world.' What does that look like?"

"You know, the nonhuman world."

I scratch my head. "You mean, humans aren't natural?"

He sits up, rekindled by territory he knows well, by brain-talk. I've never seen a people do brain-talk as well as whites. It gets them excited.

"No, well, see, we *were,* at one time. But then, then…" and he cackles a little here. "Good Lord, I'll start sounding just like my mother. I can't believe I'm incorporating religion. But there is this notion of the *fall,* and scientifically, of course, centuries of urban living, Judeo-Christian thought, Descartes…this profound ability to think."

What is he talking about? The elk don't think? They don't know where to go for grasses, or how to sniff out a lion? The mountains don't teach us that if we can take all the rockslides and floods and volcanoes, we might end up beautiful like them? And don't the trees tell us about listening? What does he mean?

"We humans are a bit on a different plane," he goes on.

I roll my eyes. Same old shit. Only now they bother to include Indians in the "human" category. Nice of them. "Luke?" I ask.

"What?"

"What's your grandmother's name."

"Eugenia Ashburn. Why?"

"Because my grandmother's name is sage."

He looks at me blankly, then gropingly. "I see. Of course." He appears proud of himself. "Nature on an equal footing. I admire that—"

"Admire it! You destroy anything natural the minute you touch it! You want it and you fear it at the same time. Just like Sarah."

"I don't know what you are talking about."

"You wouldn't." My eyes feel stitched together I'm scowling so hard. If whites like him don't kill us, then they carry around these ridiculous ideas about us. Romantic, Kit Carson said to me. White men *romanticize* the Indians. I didn't get it then, but I do now.

"Sage," I say tiredly. I pick up a clump of it from my bundle and put it in his nose. "You know, the plant that helps you breathe. Can you not see what a gift that is? What power it has?"

For a split second he looks like he wants to believe that, but he has no idea how. I feel sorry for him. So cut off from the world like that! What do whites do when they're lonely?

Then he says, "Power," almost scoffing.

I give up. "Aghh. If you don't get that sage is your grandmother, white man, you will never be an Indian."

He doesn't say anything to that. I wonder where whites think they come from, if not the sage. I wonder where his body is. Don't white people have bodies? Why don't they think their bodies have anything to say? If he listened to his body, he wouldn't be talking. He'd be breathing deep. He'd be taking lessons from the sage.

"Breathe," I say. "Breathe and be quiet."

He starts to say something but I hold up my hand. "Talking won't get you anywhere."

His face goes taut, like a mad little boy, and he starts to mutter something but stops. He takes a half breath that makes the top part of his chest move, and closes his eyes. He's back to discomfort. He wants to talk. He can't stand not talking. He can't stand being in his own body.

I stop drumming, and the flap of the door goes up.

"Well, at least you didn't bolt out of here as I thought you might," I say.

"Why would I do that?"

"'Cause you can't stand yourself. That's why."

"Look, I don't have to take this kind of ab—"

"Couldn't breathe into your gut, could you?"

"No…but what does that—"

"Why not?"

"Huh?"

"Why couldn't you breathe into your gut? Surely it's not because you have defective lungs."

Luke colors in the dark. "No," he mutters.

"Well, why not then?"

Luke doesn't answer.

"Because it didn't *feel* good, did it? Okay, Coyote, I'm gonna go get seven more rocks."

I disappear into vapors of steam and moonlight, my pitchfork periodically sticking into the lodge with another rock on the end of it. When I'm done, I crawl back to my position by the door and close the flap.

"Round two you're supposed to pray for other people. Like Sarah. Try that *and* breathing as you're supposed to in here."

Within minutes Luke is lunging for the door, but some force ejects him back over the fire and into his seat.

Great Spirit! It's all working again! I haven't seen that kind of ejection but once or twice!

This gives me renewed confidence. "Breathe," I command.

"I can't."

"Why not?"

"BECAUSE." He roars.

"Sarah," I whisper.

"No!"

"Sarah."

The name bounces through the rocks and floats on all the steam rising up around us. Pretty soon I hear weeping.

I start praying to the Great Spirit, low and out loud. I hit my deer-skin drum very softly. Bummbummbumm Bummbumm-bumm...

"Navajos have an expression," I say. "They say, 'Remember everything you have seen, for everything forgotten returns to the circling winds.'"

"Uh-nuh. What's that supposed to mean?"

"How much have you forgotten, Luke? Willed yourself to forget? Where did you leave yourself and how old were you?"

I hear hiccup noises. Is he sobbing? Is that how white men cry? Like angry donkeys?

"I love Sarah," he squeaks out between those braying sounds. Voice like a mouse, sobs like a donkey.

"You love Sarah."

"She loves me."

"She loves you." Bummbummbumm...

"Stop that fucking drum!"

"Shut up, white man. You are not in charge here."

"Oh, so is this how you get out your ya-ya's, you old dead fool? You *lost*, Ouray, your people *lost*."

I want to hurl the drum at him, I want to kill him. *Breathe, warrior. He'll see where to get you if you don't watch it.*

I let things go quiet a few minutes. Then I steer us back. "You love Sarah," I say, holding the drum tightly. Then I ask, "Do you love your wife?"

"Of course I love my wife!"

"Why did you get married?"

Luke plasters himself on the floor again, his face toward the seam. "Hot. Hot in here." He sniffs hard, brings the sage up.

"Why did you get married?"

"Because," he says, in between breathing in sage, "I wanted to make a public commitment other people would approve of."

Great Spirit. I've never seen more crazy people in my life. "What did *you* want to do? What did *your* spirit tell you to do?"

Luke sits up, puzzled. "What do you mean? That is what I wanted to do."

"Marry for image and not for love. I thought whites always married for love."

"I told you I love Cynthia!"

"Uh-huh." I throw more water on the rocks. They hiss and send up steam. I think about Lars' letter to Maddy. I think about what he said about men who would try to be "good" for some reason that had nothing to do with who they were. I sigh. "Sarah says you just like to go hiking with your students," I say.

"So? So, I go hiking." Luke sits up. He's making himself hot now. No rocks needed. He doesn't even realize that I just told him Sarah knows about me. "I always told Cynthia if she didn't want me to see them I wouldn't—"

Cynthia? I said Sarah, not Cynthia. "Ah," I say. Bummmbummmbummm…

"Ah, what?"

I hand him a bucket with a ladle and water in it. He drinks like he'd just walked a hundred miles across the desert.

"Kit Carson had an expression," I say.

"Which one is that?"

"'The path to hell is paved with good intentions.'"

"Ye-es, so?"

"Sarah…" I whisper.

"Stop it!" he mewls. And cups his hands into his stomach, gagging in a way, until I throw the flap up and cold night air overtakes him.

Into round three, and he's slobbering over there, balled up with fists burrowing his stomach like gophers, going on about his mother and a Pastor Wicks, and how Pastor Wicks was a man of God and his mother made them go to church all the time and when they were visiting just last Christmas she made them all hold hands in a circle and pray that *someone,* any one of them, would just be Born Again so that she wouldn't have to go to heaven alone.

Great Spirit.

"And Sarah doesn't do that?"

"No. Sarah loves me. Sarah does what I want. Sarah never tells me I'm bad or that I should shovel the walk—"

I want to vomit.

"Luke, why did you have relations with your daughter? Why did you do the worst thing anyone can do to their daughter?"

"I DIDN'T DO ANY SUCH THING."

"Really. Did you ever tell your mother off, either?" Elders, please forgive me. *Elders please forgive. But his mother—!*

"My mother is a perfect lady."

"Really."

His jaw's working up and down in the glow of the rocks and I just let the silence prey on him. He slaps his hands to his ears and doubles over, rocking.

"Pastor Wicks," he says.

"Pastor Wicks. What did Pastor Wicks do?"

"He—he—I can't tell you." He covers his head, balls up, tries to become invisible.

"You don't want to be seen right now, do you?"

"Go away."

"Did he do to you what you do to Sarah?"

"GO AWAY!"

The shriek echoes off the rocks, the tent wall, me.

"Pastor Wicks been circling ever since he touched you, hasn't he?" Luke rears up, lunges for me.

"Liar! Liar! I LOVE women! LOVE my mother! LOVE Cynthia!" He's slippery and long and muscled and I'm reminded of rattlesnakes grown big and long in the summer sun except for a brief few seconds when he bucks like a kicking rabbit. Great Spirit! I ratchet around, slither with him, groping for his neck, his face, his arms. I'm not afraid because I've got him, I've got him at last, this evil thing, got him wet and angry and he's Kerr, and the mine, and that Lakota brave and Nathan Meeker and the Denver *Post* screaming "The Utes Must Go!" and most of all he's that Lakota brave, again and again, that Lakota brave who took my son.

I fling him back too close to the rocks, and he stands up like lightning. "FUCKING INDIAN. YOU *LOST*, OURAY. YOU *LOST*," he shrieks.

I wince. How can he come up with that in the heat of this war? Brain like the tongue of a lizard. *Oh he's done in, he has to be done in, it's the only thing he knows to say, evil always throws blame off itself,* but he keeps screaming and I hear his screaming and feel the places where his hot flailing fists have bruised me. His words bounce through the rocks and through me. My own mind—maybe Luke's own mind—is reproducing them, echoing them in reprise. The smell of rage reaches new heights in the lodge and I start to gag. *This can't just be Luke's sweat.* For one flicker of a flame the whole lodge skews the way my tipi did the day I heard about the Meeker Massacre. The moment I heard that news I caught fire and I haven't stopped burning. I knew it was the end and I've been walking around ever since with the shadows of an entire Indian nation, dead, on my shoulders. Smallpox, measles, broken treaties, relocations, forced agriculture on ground that wouldn't grow a decent cactus, starvation, ponies shot, buffalo gone, a thousand thousand dead, gone like the pigeons that used to darken the sky there were so many of them, or the antelope that used to blanket hillsides like grass.

So much. I can't hold the loss of an entire country.

But the sweat keeps pouring out of me, as if the Great Spirit didn't care what I could or couldn't hold, what I could or couldn't contain within me. Especially my cheeks. They're soaking wet. Why are my cheeks so slick? And what is this heaving, heaving...? I lick my tongue around the sweat, and taste salt. Salt with no body odor. Just salt, so salty, salty, why? And then I realize I'm crying, I'm sobbing, each tear and heave and roil another shrouded Ute, all my relations, all, everybody, and then just Paron, Paron Paron Paron, as I knew him last, Paron at six with his scarred shoulder and boy-sized quiver, Paron Paron, cascading into the rocks.

I've lost Luke. I lose him until there's a cracking sound in the lodge, and then the stench of vomit.

We stare at each other from across the hearth. I feel I am coming back from another time and place, from very, very far away. How long have we been in this sweat? All morning? All spring? Thirty springs? The contents of our own guts lie on the ground in front of us, mine a stain of spit and tears, his a pool of vomit. The emotional racket slowly clears. I realize he's spewed up his own demons as well, which was ever my intention. I drip more water on the rocks, together with a little cedar to dampen the vomit smell.

"Good," I say, watching him. Luke's got a look like a wet, exhausted dog.

I imagine I look very nearly the same.

I keep the fourth round short. Just to let the last rocks wrap things up. We're both silent. I know he's too tired to bolt anywhere and I bet I can lead him down. We suck on sage. When the flap goes up the grey air of dawn streams in and I say, "That's it."

But he sits there a minute and says, "You know, I remember I saw another Indian like you once, I swear."

I close my eyes. Can't this be over? "You did?" I ask.

"Yes. Down Slickhorn Canyon above the San Juan. I was just going to sleep when I looked out of my bag toward the cliffs near the river, and I swear I saw a glowing Indian."

Did you piss in your pants then, too? But I don't say anything. Power medicine. This man could have been Lars, or somebody clear-headed and useful to his people, if he hadn't gotten so twisted. All that energy spent for bad. If he were a Navajo he'd shape-shift into a skinwalker and slide around the red rock country at night. At home, he just slides into his basement with his own daughter.

I recoil from him, get out of the lodge. "Don't come near me," I say, when he comes out too, the first sun slanting into the trees.

"I'm not a bad man." He's almost whimpering. "I want to be an Indian."

I sigh. "I thought we went through this."

He opens his mouth to answer but then the sound of dogs reaches us, and men's voices. He pales. I go invisible, but hold his arm behind him to make sure he won't run. "Don't move," I hiss.

He starts to protest, I can feel the words rise up in his throat. His heart pounds and finally—finally—the fear sweat breaks out of him, comes out from underneath all that rage. I relax a little, sure I was right now, sure that I did break him. Just then the dogs come up the deer path, and the men with stars on their chests. I release him.

"One last saying," I whisper, no more than the trees do.

"What's that?" Barely moving his lips in front of the men.

"'Don't compromise yourself. It's all you got.'"

I don't tell him his daughter has that on the back of her notebook. I don't say anything else. He turns and looks at me, but I've gone. I've given him back to his people, who will make up their own minds what to do with him.

Spider

Sarah

La Plata (AP) - A La Plata man wanted for sexual abuse
of children was arrested yesterday. Luke Graves, forty,
wanted on several counts, was found early yesterday
afternoon near the old mining camp of Philistine.
Smoke from a smoldering fire led authorities to the site,
after locating his car several miles below the mine. It appears
Graves was performing a sweatlodge ceremony shortly
before authorities located him…

I stop reading the paper. I'm in Miss Pike's waiting room, after
school, though I came back to the MacIntosh's early. At school I
could hardly think. I sat there and stared at my Four Corners map on
the inside flap of my notebook. Ouray, Mrs. Oodegaard, Mrs.
MacIntosh, Trent. Who was in the middle? I started drawing saggy
strands between the four lines. Around and around, spider web. Used
to be I was in the middle. But now—now it was—and the square-
jawed shape of a man began drawing itself. Square jaw, with glasses,
a geologist's hammer in his loopy fingers.

"Sarah?"

Mrs. Lovato.

"Sarah, honey, are you all right?"

I must not have been because Mrs. Lovato put an arm around my
shoulder and took me to the nurse.

Dad was in the middle. But he wasn't the spider. He was the fly.

Daddy daddy I miss you sometimes it wasn't so bad sometimes we flirted and it was okay but why wasn't it ever really okay?

There's his face, his square jaw, his ice eyes, the back of him mowing the lawn or sanding a board. There's the dad who put on Bach really loud and made a stew from scratch and no recipe on nights when Mom wasn't home. There was the dad who bought an old grey pickup truck to take stuff to the dump in that Mom thought was awful. There was the dad who took care of Beowulf when he fell out of the back of the truck and scraped his face raw on the pavement, dog skin hanging and his back leg bruised. There was the dad who was unafraid of high places or the woods, who plucked the quills from Beowulf's face when he killed a porcupine. He could do *so much.* Not like Mom, who hated camping, who got weird in church, or dizzy in crowds, and had to drive slowly on back roads to town. We never could have lived in the Rockies without Dad, and now he's caught.

I won't be allowed to see him, but I'm not sure I want to anyway. I know I don't want to see Mom. Not ever. Even if they did let her out on bail and she's back at home, waiting for some sentence for trying to push me down the stairs. Miss Pike says she has to go to counseling. She asked me how I felt about my mom and I couldn't say it but what I wanted to tell her was that I hated her guts.

Why is Dad different than that, though? Why don't I hate him? He did such bad things. It's so confusing. I write him letters almost every hour, in between my homework and assignments at school, and back at the MacIntoshes. I write letters but as soon as I put "I love you" on paper my heart squeezes and I remember all the things he did to me and maybe *that's* why Mom hates me and I hate her, and then I want to hate him, too. How could he do those things to me? How could I love him? How could he say he loved me? *Did* he love me?

When Miss Pike calls me in she sees I've got the paper and she colors a little. "Oh-oh. Shouldn't have left that out."

"Why? Why can't I see?" I'm mad. I'm sick of people hiding things from me. I tell her that.

She nods. "You're right. That's not a good thing to do. I'm sorry. I guess my first reaction is always to protect you."

"Right," I say. "Like that's protection. I'll tell you about protection. About *keeping things* from people. About not telling the *truth*." I'm so mad I could kill her.

She just stands there and takes it. Doesn't say a thing. Like she knows she's wrong.

I feel a little guilty, so I switch the subject. "So he's in jail now?" I ask.

"Yes."

"What's—what's going to happen to him?"

We sit in chairs and she says very gently, "I think he'll have to stay in jail awhile."

"Oh." I look down at my knees. My hands are twisting around on top of them. "They won't hurt him, will they?"

"No, Sarah."

We're silent a little bit. Then I decide to forgive her for wanting to hide the paper, and I start asking her all those questions. I can't sort out anything. Miss Pike finally holds her hand up to stop me from getting my tongue all tangled up and tries to explain to me that people can love other people and then turn around and hurt them a great deal. But how? I ask.

"Your father may not have been able to love with his whole heart."

"Why not? *I* love with *my* whole heart. They *told* me to be *really honest*. And to do things with a purpose. And to do things well. And—and that meant my *whole heart*." I hiccup, shouting, my face completely wet with tears and blowing my nose with about a thousand Kleenexes. "They told me to be honest. To be *honest*. And I *listened* to them." I gag at myself and slam my fists into my thighs.

Miss Pike's hands slip over my fists fast, gripping them. "Sarah," she says firmly. "Stop hurting yourself."

"Why? *They* hurt me. I must be really bad for them to hurt me like that."

"Sarah, sweetie," Miss Pike says, on her knees in front of me, one hand sweeping my hair off my face so gently I don't mind while the other holds on, still, to the fists. "It isn't about you. It's about them."

I start bawling again. "Well then I've been *had*. I've been taken for a *ride*."

"And that makes you really mad, right?"

"Ye-es. But if I wasn't bad to begin with—"

"They didn't know how to love you right because they were messed up inside about themselves."

I feel afraid again; it comes on slow, like the train into town, chugging. Even though the MacIntoshes are there I feel afraid. I haven't lived all my life with them; I don't love them the way, the way—

Of *course* Mom and Dad were all right. They had to be. Where else was I going to get supper? Clothes? A bed? If they weren't all right, well, how were me and Ricky supposed to live? They had to be all right. They had to be all right because of that, and because I loved them. *Why wasn't this good enough?* Why did it *never matter* that I loved them?

"They were very hurt people," Miss Pike says.

I shake my head. "No, it has to be me. I loved and loved and loved them and it never did any good. So there must be something about *me*. Something's *wrong* with the way I love people!" I start wailing and blow my nose again.

Miss Pike leaves her hand on my knee. "That makes you feel terrible, right?"

I nod and sniff. "Makes me want to kill myself."

"Right. And that would be terrible."

"Yeah, right."

"It would be."

"But...but..."

"Sarah, I know it's scary to think your parents might not be okay. And that they couldn't love you back. We have to believe our parents can function in the world, and that they mean what they say. We have to trust the people we love."

"So?"

"Well, but with you, they weren't all right. And you knew that."

I give her that. "Maybe. Mom always seemed like an egg about to break. And it turns out she was! She's damn Humpty Dumpty, only it's *me* who fell off the wall."

"So you kept quiet about what your dad was doing to you."

"Miss Pike, she hates me anyway. She hates being a mother. She hates herself, all tall and glasses and too smart—"

"What about your dad? What would he do if you told?"

I feel confused. Six different answers rush in at once. He'd kill me. He'd hate me. He'd really leave then because he didn't really want to be married anyway, you could see it when he was with his students. He liked me though, he really liked me better than Mom, so if I told I know he'd leave for sure. Words. Vocabulary. *Lynchpin, keystone.* I have to hold everyone together. At least I think so.

"I don't know," I say, finally. "Ricky says Dad's like cotton candy. You think you can put a finger on him and he dissolves right away."

"That's a good metaphor," says Miss Pike.

I don't say anything.

"Sarah," says Miss Pike, "look at me."

I peek out from under my bangs at her. She's still on the floor.

"What happened last week when they found the pictures? Was there a family there for you?"

I nod, barely.

Miss Pike sighs and leans back on her heels. "Remember that, Sarah. The world provides. Somehow, the world provides. You have already survived what I hope will be the worst thing you ever survive in your life."

I'm quiet a minute, then I say, "Maybe. But you still don't get it."

"Get what?"

"It's like…it's like losing a whole country. I ought to know… I've moved enough. Only it's not just to a different part of this country, or this state. It's somewhere totally new. Like Africa. And it's forever." I can feel my chin quiver and I fall apart once more.

Miss Pike tries to take my hand but I bat it away. "*You* try that, Miss Pike." I shout. "*That's* what's so bad. That's what's so bad about everything."

OURAY

"Ouray! No! You're disintegrating!"

She's back up at my crevice, touching my forearm. Pieces of it fly away in the breeze.

I'm extraordinarily sleepy. And I know I'm dissolving, going away. I can practically feel Chipeta pulling me. I haven't felt this close to her in years.

Sarah starts to cry. "Why is everyone going away from me? I don't have *anything*—I had to come back here to get my stuff and visit my mom and now she's selling the house and she looks like a ghost, and—"

But she stops when she finds herself sitting next to a glowing Indian. I can't stand it, all her crying, her loss. So I materialize for her. "I've got to go now, Sarah," I say.

"Why? And how come you can look like this now?"

She's not so much shocked at me as she is mad that I haven't showed up like this before. Her shoulders heave up and down and she fingers the paho she made last fall.

"Because," I start to say. There is no simple explanation. "Because I got rid of all the things I'd been holding onto for so many years."

"What things?"

"Grief, mainly."

"You stayed here because you felt *sad*?"

"Someday you'll understand. You see, if you don't let go of things, then you can't move onto the new thing."

"How do you know when it's time to let go?"

I'm silent on this one for a minute. "When you can stand to, I think," I finally say.

Now she's quiet, sniffing and wiping her sleeve across her nose and still crying.

"I don't think I can stand anything," she says.

I touch her cheek. "You've had it hard," I say.

She nods. Either she's too shocked to feel it strange that I would know about her life, or she doesn't care.

In the back of a crevice is a basket I was buried with. It has stood up to time because it's very dry back there and my body was blocking the wind. "Here," I say to her. "This is for you."

She looks astonished. "But this is so old! It's worth a fortune! It's yours!"

I shake my head. "No. It would have been my son's. But he grew up not knowing who he was. That won't happen to you. I made sure of it. So next time you can't stand anything, put your feelings in here."

"What? Why?"

"Because it will hold them for you. That's what I've decided we all need to do. Find something big enough to hold all our feelings. So it's safe to have them. So you don't split in two the way your dad did." I almost say, the way I did, but I forgive myself a little bit. I might have terrorized Lars, but there are levels of depravity and mine wasn't near Luke Graves'. "That was his whole problem, you know," I go on. "I think somebody hacked into him with an ax and he never could stand how much it hurt. So he kept part of himself permanently axed and that rage had to go out somewhere. Evil happens, I think, when the right hand doesn't know what the left hand is doing."

"How do you know so much about my dad?"

I shut up. But she's got it figured out by the look on her face. "*You* were the spider!" she says.

"Huh?"

"The paper said he was next to a sweatlodge. Poles and fire and everything. *You* did that."

"Well, maybe…" Great Spirit, there is no fooling this girl. The Spirit's still grinning at me, pleased as a coyote with fresh rabbit for having gotten all those tears out of me. Got you, Ouray, finally, It says, every time the oak leaves dance in the sun, or the meadowlarks start fluting. Got you.

Sarah sighs. "It's okay, I guess. I mean, that you were the one who got him. Somebody else might have killed him, by mistake or whatever. People who run from the cops sometimes get shot."

I don't exactly know what "the cops" are but I assume it's the law. I nod my head. "Sometimes."

Sarah fingers the basket. "Did Chipeta make this?"

"Yes," I say.

"It's beautiful."

We look out over the valley together. Then she gazes down into the basket.

"I think God is this," she says.

"What?"

"That's what God has to be anymore. Not some horrible man who judges you from heaven, but something big enough to hold everything you are."

Now I really can't stand it. I can't stand how wise she is. And how much pain is behind that wisdom.

"Ah, shit, Sarah."

"What? What'd I do?"

"Nothing," I say, knuckling her skull, moving close. I smell her little girl smell, a clean soapy scent. I squeeze my eyes to stop my own tears. "Take care of yourself."

"Wait—!"

"I'm always in your dreams, you know that." And I wink out, leaving her with my flaking bones, and the basket, woven tightly, gripped between her hands.

Weavers

Trent's dad finds out about Joe Peterman and me the day he takes all four of us kids to the hardware store. Joe's in there, buying nails, and Trent's trailing behind, being nice to me one minute, kind of mad the next. I told him about Chief Ouray last night and I think it bugs him.

"Howdy, Joe," his dad says. "I have some work for you if you're interested."

"How long? I gotta cabinet job next week."

"Just two days or so."

Joe nods. "Okay." He looks at me and Ricky and Brandon and Trent. "What're you doing here?" he asks me.

Trent looks at me weird again. His dad looks at Joe. This is fun. When I went with Dad, we never said hello to anybody. "You know her?" his dad asks.

"Yeah. Comes in the bar, that one does. Wants to learn to play the blues."

Now everybody's staring at me and Trent's dad asks, "Do your parents take you to places like that?"

"No," I scowl. But then I look down at the floor. "Said, um, I was going to the library. While my mom got her hair cut."

"Oh brother," Trent mumbles, but his dad's mouth is twitching like he secretly loves a mischief-maker.

"I'll be damned. You didn't get her drunk, did you, Joe?"

Joe snorts. "Yeah, right. Naw, all I did was teach her *Rocket 88*. That a sin?"

"No," says Mr. MacIntosh. "I guess not."

Joe opens a sack and puts nails inside. "I'll tell you what's a sin, MacIntosh. What's a sin is you don't play with us anymore."

Trent scowls at his dad like he's puzzled, and my eyes bug out. "You play?" I ask. "What do you play?"

"Yeah, Dad." Brandon pipes in. "What do you play?"

Even Ricky's interested. But MacIntosh's fuming. "Oh Goddammit, Joe. You know, if you kept your trap shut just once in your life it would be a great sign of growth."

"He plays banjo. Really well."

"*Banjo.*" I'm ecstatic. I told Dad I wanted to play banjo once but he just gave me the same old story about learning classical first. "Oh, please, Mr. MacIntosh, will you teach me?" I grab his hand without even thinking. Something softens in Mr. MacIntosh; I can see his arm slouch, but Trent grabs his other arm just as fast and throws a mean look at me.

Trent's dad looks down at us. He squeezes Trent's hand and brings it up to his side as if he were trying to tell him he still loves him best, I think, and Trent kind of puffs up. It makes me sad 'cause he's right; his dad should love Trent better.

But his dad still answers me. "Yeah, maybe I'll teach you." He throws a gruff look at Joe. "See what trouble you get me in?"

"And Ricky," I go on, "Ricky plays ragtime like you've never seen."

Joe's eyes walk to Ricky, who's standing stalk-still and listening to every word. Ricky blushes. "You do?" Joe asks. Ricky nods. "Well, Mac, looks like we got ourselves a regular band." Joe's mouth can barely keep from cracking a grin. "Bring that banjo down along with these kids some afternoon."

"Oh for God's sake, Peterman."

But Joe's eyes twinkle out from his fat cheeks like two blue stars. "When'd you say you wanted me over to work?"

Mr. MacIntosh sighs. "Tomorrow. I want you tomorrow. Nine o'clock."

"Will do." Joe whistles and walks to the checkout line.

Trent's dad turns to the rows of screws and nails in little bins in front of him. He looks at them sort of dumb, then at Brandon, and then Trent. "What'd we come in here for, son?" he asks Trent.

Trent just rolls his eyes.

MADDY

I'm standing out in the front yard admiring the view and feeling a little sorrowful for the family next door when Ouray appears. We don't even say hello, just nod as if it were the most natural thing in the world that a ghost from the nineteenth century would show up right then. I notice he takes in the valley as I do, but then looks away as if it still causes too much pain.

"Good work with Luke Graves," I say, more to make him feel good than anything else.

"You knew it was me?"

I nod. "They said he surrendered without much of a fuss." I turn to look at him head-on, over my glasses. "They also said he'd been in a sweatlodge."

"Funny. Sarah picked that up, too. He didn't say he'd been in there with me, did he?"

I laugh. "Luke Graves? Admit to spending time with the ghost of Chief Ouray? I don't think so. It didn't make the paper, at any rate."

"Well, in that case, here." He smiles in a hangdog way and lays a torn set of sheets and several blankets at my feet.

I bat a hand at his golden countenance. "I knew you took them."

He smiles but he still seems sad. I figure there is so much he wants to say, about Graves, about a society that produces men like Graves, about the valley chewed up and fenced in front of him, looking love-ly but probably not half so lovely as what he remembers.

"What'd it look like before we whites came?" I ask, softly.

"What? The valley?"

I nod.

He scans it, settling on the plain where some horses graze. "No barbed wire," he says.

"That's it?"

He shakes his head. "Of course not." The corners of his eyes seem to have withered even further. "No fields cut for hay. No houses. Just maybe the smoke from a campfire. Lots of elk come winter. Frogs. Tribes full of them when the snows melted and all the ponds and things filled up."

A chainsaw sounds in the far distance. His head shifts with the noise. "Oh," he says, "one other thing. Silence. So you could hear what the magpie had to say. Or the elk. Or anybody. It was nice."

I find myself smiling as bittersweetly as he is.

He clears his throat, fingering a war bonnet. It is long and cascades with bright feathers. I glance at it, wanting to touch it but not daring to. "What now for you, Mrs. Oodegaard?" he asks.

I have to smile. I'm probably the only white person he could ever muster that much care for, except maybe Sarah. "I'm not sure, Chief. I've been sleeping better this past week."

"Have you dreamt of Lars?" he asks.

"No-o, I don't think so. I haven't dreamt much at all lately. Why?"

He shrugs his shoulders. "Just curious."

We keep silent for a minute. A gush of air sings through the pines behind us, and then he says, "Well, I just wanted to say goodbye." He's standing there with the war bonnet, and he's looking at me full in the face for the first time. Then he turns back to the valley, as if he can't make up his mind whether it's worse to stay or worse to say goodbye, finally, after all these years and all that struggle.

"This is a huge goodbye for you," I say.

To my surprise, his chin caves in and the tears streak his brown impassive cheeks. "I saw Chipeta," he says, his voice a scratch. "She's waiting for me."

"Good," I say.

"Now maybe you can find Lars," he says.

"Maybe."

"When you find him, say hello for me, will you?"

"Certainly."

"I've learned a great deal from both of you."

"You have? About what?" I can't imagine what a great Indian chief who has lived to see so many heartbreaking changes would see in the two of us.

He thinks a minute, his mind working for words. Then he says, "Well, I suppose love, Mrs. Oodegaard. What you whites call love."

And then he's gone, as fast as he came, the golden, fringed glow that was Ouray vanishing to his beloved spirit land at last. I can only stand there stupidly, gazing out at the valley like a cow, silently thrilled to find I've had some profound use in the world after all.

BARBARA

"You know, Madeleine, you are looking brighter these days."

We're out at Mesa Verde. Trent said he had something to do with the kids today, something with Joe Peterman. I didn't ask because I assume it involves fishing. So Maddy and I came here, spent the morning in the museum. But now we're done and we've parked ourselves at the Sun Temple, on the mesa top. The remnants of lunch sit on a nearby picnic table. It's warm, a June Saturday, with thunderheads in the far distance.

"Why, thank you, Barbara, I do feel better," Maddy says. Magpies spin out of a juniper. "Gorgeous day."

"Yes. Thank God. That was the longest winter of my life."

Maddy turns her face toward the late morning sun. She puts a hand on my arm the way she did so many months ago when she wanted to give her condolences about Trent. "Not even the winter after your father's death?" she asks.

I spill a little soda. "Why, you remember that!"

"Of course. I knew both your parents well. You moved away after that, if I recall."

"Yes. To Colorado Springs. My mother taught school."

"But you came back here."

"Yes."

She doesn't talk for a bit, takes a stroll up to the walls of the Sun Temple. It's a circular structure, probably ceremonial, restored out of cement and sandstone to an approximation of its former glory. God knows if it's accurate. A lot of the restoration dates to the 1930s, and the work of the CCC.

Maddy puts her arms on top of a wall. "Your father loved it here, loved Four Corners country," she says.

"I know."

"Is that why you came back?"

I don't look at her. But suddenly the air hums thick with him, with love, the juniper fragrant in the growing sun and the smell and taste of dust so familiar. "Yes," I manage to say. I remember the countless camping trips, the one we were on when the Jeep overturned, all of us in it with him but spilling out, all except him, stuck somehow between steering wheel and pedals, the Jeep pivoting on a boulder— but I stop that. I've been over and over that territory, the territory of sudden accident and terrible silence, of wheels spinning fruitlessly in air. I reach for a juniper. "He taught me to love it too," I say, plucking a berry and putting it in my mouth.

Maddy's beside me again. "I figured as much."

"That was his greatest gift. Because this land is big enough to hold any pain you can imagine."

Maddy smiles. "Somebody once informed me that among the many lessons to be learned from this place, one of the best was that it was possible to incorporate great pain, great upheaval—to be full of wretched, ugly stories, stories of burning and volcanoes and floods— and turn out beautiful because of them. Those stories give us our shape."

I turn to her. "Who told you that?"

She pulls a berry down for herself, not looking at me. "Man named Chief Ouray."

"Ouray! Sarah told Trent about him too. What's with Chief Ouray?"

But Maddy just grins and sucks her berry. "You know," she says, pulling it out, "they flavor gin with these." And she pops it back in her mouth, trying to bite it gently, so as to get a little of the puckery juice.

SARAH

The first ever meeting of the La Plata Rag and Blues Time Band happens at the Kittredge at two p.m. the day after school gets out for the summer. I never noticed before, but a big old painting of Ouray hangs over the bar in the Kittredge. I wink at him now, but I feel sad too. I wish he'd come back.

Ricky spies the upright and gets excited. All his ragtime fantasies are about to come true. He races to the bench, sits down, and rattles off a Scott Joplin before anybody can stop him. Mr. MacIntosh just gapes at him.

"Aw, hell," he swipes a paw in the air. "I can't keep up with *that.*"

"Sure you can, MacIntosh," growls Joe. "It's just been a while."

Trent stands quiet, next to me. I can feel his arm touching mine, lengthwise, and even though I don't dare take it, I'm so glad that he doesn't remove it. I couldn't stand it if he was mad at me forever.

Trent's been kind of forced into coming here, though. He's supposed to be an audience, along with Brandon, and maybe a percussion player, and he fussed the whole way down in the car. You'd think he'd be happier because his face looks better ever since they did some surgery a couple weeks ago. They flew him to Galveston and everything.

"All right," says Joe. "We got two or three piano players, depending on if you count me, a banjo player, and a guitar player. That's me also. So, seeing as how no one else plays guitar, I guess I'll play that."

He hoists himself up on the stage, pulls his instrument from behind the curtain, and sits next to Ricky. "Know any blues?" he asks.

Ricky shakes his head. "That's okay. You will."

Mr. MacIntosh plucks at his banjo as Ricky plays another rag. He plucks lightly, so no one but himself will hear I guess, but soon his foot is tapping and his confidence is growing and the banjo just gets louder. Then *The Entertainer* becomes a two-instrument piece, really well-played, and even Stoney the barman stops stocking glasses to listen.

"Nice," says Stoney, when they're done.

"Great," mumbles Joe. "That's one piece at least two of us know."

"It's true. We don't have much of a repertoire," says Trent Sr.

"Well, we'll get one." Joe puts a glance toward me. "First, I gotta teach this girl the blues. We'll have a blues pianist and a ragtime pianist. A blues guitarist and a ragtime banjo man. Two bands in one. And whoever's not playing can do percussion stuff or something for the other."

"All right, then," says Trent Sr. "Sounds like a plan." But he's not really hearing. He's sidled up next to Ricky and begun another banjo tune. Ricky listens for a minute and starts plucking it out on the piano.

Joe, Trent, Brandon and me look on in the dusky dust-mote air of the saloon. "Ricky always did have a great ear," I say.

Joe shrugs. A big paw goes down on both Trent and my shoulders. "Screw 'em. We'll come back when they're not so busy with themselves."

"What do we do now?" asks Trent.

"Well," says Joe, "your daddy just paid me for that work of his. I say we go get ice cream."

BARBARA

When we drive into town from Mesa Verde, I swear I hear banjo floating in through my car window. Trent Sr. played banjo, but he quit some time ago. I never did ask him why, though my dad played it too and I used to cry when Trent Sr. played it. So maybe he didn't want to make me sad, but I always loved it when he took it up. When Trent was first born, he used to sing him to sleep with Doc Watson tunes, played very softly.

We pass the train depot, Safeway, gas stations, the fairground with its long adobe wall of horse stalls. We go north out of town on the other side, up the valley toward Maddy's house, Sarah's.

"Sarah and Ricky see Carole Pike every week," I say.

"She's the counselor, right?"

I nod.

"So what does Carole Pike say about the Graves family?"

"Um, it's delicate right now. I think Cynthia Graves has to make some amends. Maybe someday she'll get her kids back. But right now she's not very stable."

"Is she getting help?"

I nod. "Yes. I guess the plan is to get them all together, or at least the mother with the kids, for some serious counseling."

"I'll say. I wouldn't want that woman back with her children, ever. What about jail?"

I look at Maddy. "Not much sympathy, eh?"

"A woman who lets that sort of thing go on in her own house and then tries to throw her daughter down the stairs for it…!"

"Well, she's out on bond. Maybe the judge will feel as you do."

We're quiet a minute. Maddy's head turns to look out toward the east side of the valley, the red cliffs with their distant ponderosa and the thunderheads piling up in the middle of a royal blue sky. I think I hear sniffling. "Are you crying?" I ask.

She turns toward me, old face, plump, wrinkled, with wire rim glasses. "Yes."

I don't say anything. She goes on. "It's just…my children were my pride and joy. My pride and joy. And Lars' too, for all his troubles. How can you treat them…?"

I put my arm on hers this time. "No need to explain. I've dreamt through thoughts like that for nights now."

We pass Sarah's house and pull into Maddy's driveway. Maddy looks at her neighbor's. "It's for sale," she says. "What about money? What will she do? The kids?"

"She can teach," I say. "They'll probably leave once things stabilize, she does her penance, and she can work again."

Maddy looks at me. "How does that make you feel?"

"Not good. I don't know what Trent'll do without Sarah."

"How about what you will do?"

The question comes softly, a gentle pat of rain. I buckle on a small rise of tears.

"I don't know."

In the rinse of dawn, the dishwater time after the stars fade, I lie awake. The Jeep wheels are spinning. They spin and spin, up in the air above dewy nettles and green summer grass and the sparkly granite of boulders. Nobody has to tell me there's a man pinned underneath.

Sarah said something to me last night, crying and rubbing a heart-shaped piece of sandstone with her fingers. She said: *I lost my best friend.* She was talking about her dad, that absent father, that geologist who rapes, that man. And I saw it all then, bits of sandstone crumbling onto her knees—all the splits and ratcheting and the mangled shape of her poor heart. Because I knew what it was like to lose a father who was, in whatever way it happened, your dearest friend on earth. (Was it inevitable that daughters loved their fathers so? That fathers were their best friends no matter what the circumstances, because we *wanted* them to be so much?) My father drank too much, probably, and my mother and he had their troubles, and he worked sixty hours a week. But he was still my best friend, still the only one who could take my hand and walk through a meadow to go fishing. The only one who would go out with me on a cold autumn night to stare at the stars. We knew each of the constellations in each of the seasons, Orion orbiting with his belt around the universe as the months spun by. He saved dirty jokes he heard in the courtroom just for me, saved them for those constellation nights when Mom was asleep or inside putting the dishes away. We had a cabin up on the road to Telluride and we'd birdwatch for hours, seeking out bald eagles hunting fish along the Dolores River, waiting in the willows for the redwing blackbirds to land above our heads and stake out territory. Just like Sarah, in a way, who tells me how she would collect rocks off the mountain behind her house, and he would identify all the minerals within them. She knows feldspar, mica, quartz. She has a shoe box full of gypsum, quartz crystals, shimmering pyrite. Some of them he brought back for her from trips, some she found.

So at the rinsewater hour, I see Jeep wheels spinning in midair. My equivalent of Sarah's recurrent dream of a sweatlodge, an Indian (Ouray?), and men with handcuffs, clamping down on her father's wrists and taking him away forever.

"Let's take these strips and make a potholder," Maddy says. The strips smell like a campfire and each of the kids has a glass of lemonade in front of them on the dining room table. School's been out three weeks and Maddy's been over several times since. I smile and fade into the background, watching a few minutes from the far end of the kitchen, where Beowulf lies curled and asleep.

"What's this from, an old bedsheet?" Ricky asks.

"Yes, actually," Maddy says.

"Why does it smell like a fire?" Trent's got his crooked fingers wrapped around a strip, wrestling it onto the plastic potholder board they just bought at Woolworth's. I cringe a little at his struggle, just the way I did watching him make the split-twig figurine earlier this spring. But he does it easier now, so the improvement bolsters me. So much plasticity—doctor-word—is compromised by burn scars.

Yes, doctor, whatever you say. And Sarah—Sarah says she wants to learn how to make a basket. She comes in and watches me sometimes, glides into the room without a word and sits down next to my loom or my chair.

"I want a basket with the peaks on the rim, just the way they rim La Plata," she said, yesterday. "We could make a circle of pointed triangles to represent the peaks."

"And what about below the peaks?"

"Some tree shapes, maybe? And around the bottom, a squiggly line."

"What'll that be for?"

"The river, Mrs. MacIntosh. What else?"

I smile, thinking about that. I decide to join everyone at the table with its strips of woodsmoke bedsheets in the center. I've got a pen and a piece of paper. I draw a circle. Grass on my bottom ring. Peaks on top, like Sarah. But in the middle? A Jeep? No, no. Shake my head. Tilt it. Turn the paper.

"Whatcha making?" Brandon asks.

He's next to me, fiddles with his belt—too long, but with a cowboy buckle he has been wanting forever. I look down at it, smile.

"Nothing," I say, and start drawing Orion, traipsing around and around between peaks and grass, always with me, always.

SARAH

"Weaving a basket is like weaving your notebook web, only a bit more complex," Mrs. MacIntosh says to me.

"What web?" Trent asks.

I get up and go to the room me and Ricky sleep in. I pull my notebook off the shelf, where it's sat since school got out, and take it back into Mrs. MacIntosh's weaving room.

"Here," I say, opening it.

Trent squints at it. "What're those names under the web lines?"

"Uh, you and your mom and Mrs. Oodegaard and, um, Chief Ouray."

"Mom, Sarah says Chief Ouray's a skeleton behind her house and—"

"I know. You told me."

My face feels like the color of the desert when the sun goes down. Mrs. MacIntosh must really think I'm nuts now. First she knows I love my sick Dad, now this.

"Well, what if she does think that?" Trent asks.

Mrs. MacIntosh shrugs from her loom. "So?"

"Well, people who think like that are usually crazy."

"Is Sarah crazy?"

Trent looks at me, then grins. "Yes," he says. I swat at him and chase him from the room.

BARBARA

"Okay, Sarah, you started your web with four stays. The Four Corners lines. That's good, but with a basket we usually need more." I pull eight or so sturdy strands of willow from a large basket. Trent stretches his neck to see.

"Come around here, Trent, you can see better. If you want to watch, that is."

He pouts. "Yes. I wanna watch."

I throw him a look. "You do? You never wanted to before."

He pulls his mouth in as much as he can and says, "I just want to."

I glance at Sarah. "Will you excuse us a minute?"

Sarah nods, and leaves the room.

"Trent, are you still jealous of Sarah?"

He rubs one toe against the other. "No."

"Look at me, babe."

He lifts his chin and gazes at me. I laugh. "Ever the stubborn one, aren't you?"

"No," but he's trying to put out a smile.

I kneel and bury my face in his neck. He smells so good, so little boy. "Trent, why don't you just tell me how you really feel about all this?"

He is quiet a minute before answering. "'Cause it's all confusing," he says. His hands rest on my back, lightly.

"In what way?"

"Well, one minute I like Sarah a whole bunch. The next she bugs me."

"How does she bug you?"

"All that weird talk about Ouray and stuff. And Four Corners maps, and playing piano at the Kittredge with Joe Peterman."

"She does that?"

"You didn't know?"

"I'll be damned. Is that where your dad took you a couple weekends ago?"

"Mo-om!" Trent glares at me as if I'd just stolen a donut or something. "If I hung out in bars by myself you'd have a cow! God. Dad acted just the same as you did."

I wipe the smile off my face but inside I'm just beaming. My husband, off doing music again. And with the kids! "You're right, I would," I say. "But, is that really why she bugs you? All those things she does that are maybe a little strange? Or are you mad because she takes up my attention?"

He doesn't say anything but he knows I know I've got it right. I sit back up on my weaving stool. "Trent, would I ever abandon you?"

I know he doesn't have to think about that one but he waits a minute just for the sake of argument. "No," he mutters, finally.

"Well, then. You know how it feels to be that hurt, as hurt as Sarah. Can you feel that for Sarah, too, or do you just feel jealousy?"

"I do feel, Mom, I do! That's the problem."

I'm puzzled. Trent twists his hands. "See, Mom," he says, "what happens is I know *exactly* how she feels sometimes and sometimes I know she knows *exactly* how I feel and I, you know, *love* her then. But then I think if I love her like this, you must too. And I can't stand that."

"Because then you're afraid I would love her more than you?"

He nods, looking at the floor again.

I slide back down and kiss his cheek. "Trent, honey, what you and

Sarah have is really special. I can't feel what you feel."

"Why not?"

"Because I've never been as hurt as either one of you."

"So you don't love her?"

"No, I wouldn't say that. But I—look, what you feel for Sarah is yours. No one else's. Not even mine."

Trent seems to slowly realize he likes this. I can tell by his expression. It's all his, his feelings for Sarah, his relationship with her.

"So what do you feel for me?" he asks.

"Oh, Trent, honey," I say, throwing my arms around him again. "You're my firstborn. My son. I love you more than you will ever know."

He can't resist one last question. "More than Brandon?"

I hold him at arm's length and catch the mischief in his eye. "Oh, get out of here," I say. "You're just like your dad."

He grins then, and leaves me to my rug, half built along the loom.

Earthsong

The snow geese tell us how they decided to make dancing haloes around the two children as they walked to the park on that high, house-ridden mesa above town. The sun was sharp, spectacular. The geese tell us they swooped and dove, sometimes right through the children's hearts and out the other side. The little boy seemed ethereal, they say, almost beautiful in his ugliness. The elastic mask is off now, and while one side of his face is only mildly scarred, the other side is a flesh-colored mudslide, a slump of skin and scar tissue. The red of the underside of his eye is still a little bit visible despite surgery, and the mouth caves and puckers into a permanent frown. But his cheekbones are intact, and his eyes have lost none of their expressiveness. That morning his eyes were bright, so bright that the geese couldn't help but skid from them, wings flapping.

Then, they tell us, this happened: a small, twisted hand slipped into the normal hand of the little girl. She took it, and choked. The two of them stopped in the street. She cried and cried, and Trent, tentatively, looking around to ensure that no other boys would see him, put his other gnarled clump of fingers to her hair.

We've followed the two of them with the utmost curiosity. They hike up here one day, midsummer, with Trent's parents. The two younger brothers skip along as well, but it's Trent and Sarah we want to know about most. How do you carry your scars? We want to ask them, but the geese tell us that in fact, they are here to ask that of us. All two-leggeds are. To them, say the geese, we look magnificent. In town they sell colorful likenesses of us, snow-capped or flanked with new green aspen, for visiting two-leggeds to send to other two-leggeds who've never seen us. We're considered beautiful and powerful.

Interesting, we say. We've never thought of ourselves as something beautiful. Massive perhaps, lofty, but not particularly beautiful. We know the scars inside; we know that the dikes of schists are exactly the same thing as Trent's swirled skin, as whatever pain Sarah sleeps with at night. But now, looking at those two children, those small two-leggeds with the swirls inside and out, the scars forming and re-forming and healing over, we see how beautiful they are.

When no one is looking, Sarah slips a basket out of her little backpack and tucks it among some of our loose rock. This is for you, she says, I made it. It's for you because you see everything and protect me. See? See the rim with the triangles? That's you. That's you, the peaks. Every day I look at you, and it helps.

The last of the snowmelt weeps out of our rocks at her gift. She splays her hand against a new-wet rock, shiny in the sun. She smiles.

Trent comes and finds her. He doesn't ask what she's been doing. A riverine compassion courses between them. It's so deep we're stunned.

The geese feather onto our shoulders.

You know what else is a basket? they say.

No, what else?

Words, this story.

Why?

Because without it all would be silent, and Sarah would still be splitting in two at the hands of her father. Silence kept him alive.

Ah. We see.

And clack a few rocks down the cliffs, just to make noise. Just to make our own voice. While the two-leggeds laugh at a joke we've missed, and the geese, the geese flutter and coo, dancing with threads of the sun.